PACO'S MIRACLE

by Ann Nolan Clark

Illustrated by Agnes Tait

Paco loved the lonely place in the mountains where he and the Old One lived. They had each other, but all the animals were Paco's friends. They followed him around, wanting to be with him, and knowing he would never hurt them. The Old One told him over and over that it was his heritage to live the gentle life and be kind to all things. The only one who remained wild to him was a dog, and even he followed Paco everywhere, but wouldn't make friends. The Old One became ill and Paco had to have him brought down the mountain and taken to Santa Fe to be cared for. All the townspeople wanted to keep Paco, but he went to live with Tómas and his bride in a new house, a new experience after living in the forest. He almost, but not quite, forgot his mountain home, but when the animals called to him, he went back and made the whole village happy with the gifts of the forest.

Classification and Dewey Decimal: Fiction (Fic)

About the Author:

ANN NOLAN CLARK began her work as a teacher in government schools for Indians of the Southwest. She became a specialist in Indian education and helped establish schools and train teachers both here and in Central and South America. She was a delegate to UNESCO conferences in Brazil and in Paris. She received the Distinguished Service Award of the Department of the Interior, the Newbery Medal and the Regina Medal of the Catholic Library Association for her contribution to children's literature.

About the Illustrator:

AGNES TAIT is well known as a portrait and mural painter as well as a book illustrator. Her work has been exhibited nationally and her lithographs are in the permanent collections of the Metropolitan Museum and the Library of Congress. Mrs. Tait's home is in Santa Fe, New Mexico.

PACO'S MIRACLE

by *Ann Nolan Clark*

ILLUSTRATED BY AGNES TAIT

1968 FIRST CADMUS EDITION
THIS SPECIAL EDITION IS PUBLISHED BY ARRANGEMENT WITH
THE PUBLISHERS OF THE REGULAR EDITION
FARRAR, STRAUS & GIROUX, INC.
BY
E. M. HALE AND COMPANY
EAU CLAIRE, WISCONSIN

Library of Congress Catalog Card Number 62-7326

Published simultaneously in Canada
by Ambassador Books, Ltd., Toronto.

This edition lithographed in U.S.A. by Wetzel Brothers, Inc., Milwaukee, Wisconsin

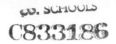

PACO'S MIRACLE

IT was night, black night. There was no moon.
There were no stars. Paco wakened. He sat up, pulling
the thin blanket around his shoulders. The ground
beneath him was cold. The night around him was cold
with the first hint of autumn.

Something had wakened him. He looked around in
the darkness. He could see nothing. He listened. He
could hear nothing. All the night noises of the high
places were stilled for the moment.

The boy got up from his blanket bed. Quietly he
crept to the opening of the lean-to where he slept.
There was no spark in the campfire in the center of
the clearing. Hours ago the last ember had burned to
ashes. The mountain top was very still. Nothing
stirred. Nothing moved. The whole world seemed
wrapped in heavy, waiting silence.

Paco shivered, not with cold. He was used to mountain chill. He shivered, perhaps from fear. He did not
know. Usually he was not afraid. All the animals and
birds of the mountain top were his neighbors. He
knew them. He did not fear them. The Old One was

his family. The Old One? This was what had wakened him. Something was wrong with the Old One. He had fear for the Old One's welfare.

Quickly the boy walked to the old man's lean-to on the other side of the clearing. In the darkness he could see the darker form on the ground. The old man lay huddled in his blanket.

"Pierre," the young boy whispered. "Pierre, Old One, what is wrong? How can I help you?"

The question brought a flood of words from the old man's lips. "Three families—French—all from Briançon —all with the same dream. Boy, do you understand?"

"I understand, Pierre," the boy answered. "I know what you tell me. You have told me many times before."

But the old man kept on talking. "We had a settlement . . . a new kind of life . . . in a new world . . . everything was good. . . . You must not forget . . . you have the heritage . . . of our dream. . . ."

Paco knelt on the ground. He put his hand on the Old One's face. It was burning with fever. Fear held the boy's heart. What should he do?

He went outside to the campfire, fumbled in the darkness for kindling and matches. Soon he had a small fire burning. Its flame cheered him. Its crackling comforted him. He made a hot drink of water and cornmeal. But the old man would not drink. He wanted only to talk.

His voice went on and on, on and on, words hurrying after words. The boy tried not to listen. He knew the story well. He could say it word by word. He had heard it so many times.

The Old One had come from Briançon, high in the French Alps, bordering Italy. He had come young, strong, longing for adventure. He had come to make a new life in the New World. In Canada the young Pierre had joined a band of French trappers. They were men of courage and daring. They roamed the wilderness, hunting and trapping. They went southward, following the fur animals. For many years Pierre had roamed with them. He had led them into new adventures. He loved the wild, free life.

Then suddenly in the mountains of Taos the Old One had changed.

Paco did not know what had made him change. He knew only that the Old One had turned his back on the life of a bold fighting trapper. He had turned away from the torture of trapping and the cruelty of killing. He had vowed to live the rest of his days in friendship with all wild creatures.

The Old One had always been a leader. He had led the trappers in wilderness living. Now he determined to lead them into a life of gentleness to God's creatures.

Three Frenchmen, all from Briançon, had listened to him. They had followed him into a quiet valley. They had brought their families. They planted vineyards on the sunny mountain slope. They planted poplars on the banks of the mountain river. They built a church and chose as their patron Saint Francis of Assisi. This was not a difficult choice. As boys they had loved the Saint. He had walked across the mountains from Italy to preach to their countrymen. His mother had been French as they were French.

Five hundred, six hundred years ago, the Saint had come to their country. But time did not matter. Saint Francis had preached to their people. Now in the wilderness of the New World, these men from Briançon would follow his teachings. They would choose his way of life—a life of kindness to all creatures.

Paco's thoughts were interrupted. The Old One began to talk again "Not His will," he said, "not God's will. Not a bit of Old France—not here. I have told you —what happened."

"Yes, Pierre," Paco answered. The Old One had told him. Paco relived the story. Snow had come to the French settlement in the valley. Day after day after day it had fallen, covering everything. Then the night of the blizzard had come, the night of the big winds, the night of the snow slide. By morning, when at last the sun shone down into the valley, there was nothing there. The church was gone. The vineyards and trees were gone. The houses and the people were gone, all except Pierre and the baby Paco.

How long ago it had been Pierre had never been certain. Nine years, ten years, he did not know. He knew only that he had escaped. He knew only that he carried the small boy of his neighbor and countryman. He could not remember how long it had taken him. He knew only that he had ploughed through the snow across the mountains and two valleys.

At last he had reached a settlement. The Spanish people there had welcomed him and the boy he carried. They had urged him to stay and be one of them.

The old Frenchman would not listen to them. He would not stay with them. Springtime had come and he had gone to the mountain top to clear a home for himself and the boy.

The dream of his French settlement in the New World was not to be. He was not to lead his countrymen in the gentle life. In a night it had gone forever. But something of the dream remained. The boy was left to him. He would teach this boy the way of kindness to all things. He would teach this boy to walk in the footsteps of Saint Francis. Then he could lead other men to the gentle life.

Paco knew this. He knew the Old One wanted him

to walk in the footsteps of the Saint. It was all the Old One ever talked about. The boy wanted to do all that the old man expected of him.

But he wondered if he could do it. Could he do what the Saint had done? Would the birds and the animals listen to him? They were not afraid of him. Paco knew this. But did they love him? Did they understand when he spoke to them? Paco did not know. This was the heaviness that he carried in his heart. He thought of it now in the stillness of the mountain top.

Paco went back into the lean-to. He did not know what to do. He felt frightened and alone.

The old man seemed to sense the young boy's fear. At last he said, "Go for help. I am very ill. Go down into the town. Get to the house of the Padre. Tell him I sent you. He will know what to do."

Paco knew the town in the valley below the mountain top. He had gone down the mountain trail once each month for as long as he could remember. He loved the quiet little town. He liked the quiet, friendly people. He knew the Padre. The old priest always smiled and spoke to him.

But he did not go. He stood looking down at the Old One huddled in his blanket. Pierre, asking for help? Pierre, the independent one, calling for the Padre?

Then Pierre began to mumble again, words without meaning, "Saint Francis . . . you must not forget. . . ."

12

Paco came to life. He ran from the lean-to, stopping only long enough to smother the campfire. The mountain top was filled with grey dawn. The valley town lay still in sleeping darkness.

The boy went swiftly down the narrow trail. He went quietly, sure-footed and fearless. A deer bounded by him. Something crashed in the underbrush. Strange eyes gleamed at him from the bushes, like trapped fireflies held motionless.

He walked swiftly, lightly, quietly. Tree roots across the trail did not trip him. Stones did not rattle as his bare feet touched them. He was mountain-trained.

Santa María-of-the-Gardens lay below him at the foot of the mountain. Santa María-of-the-Gardens was a pretty town, old and timeworn. Its four streets began at the plaza. They were crooked streets, narrow, dusty, paved with river stones. The river stones were smooth, worn smooth by many feet and many years.

All the 'dobe houses at the sides of the street were whitewashed with gypsum. All the doors of all the houses were painted with blue paint. All the small house yards were overcrowded with gardens of autumn flowers.

In the plaza the old Church of Santa María guarded its people. It had been guarding them for two hundred years or more. Facing the church across the plaza was the House of Government. It was old, too, as old as the church.

14

The schoolhouse and the store were new. They had been built when the grandfathers of the town were boys.

The post office in a corner of the store was very new. It was as new as the United States flag that hung over its doorway. The people were proud of the flag. Their Alcalde had sent to Santa Fe for it. When he gave it to them he had said, "There is talk that the States will fight among themselves. We must show the flag to show our loyalty."

The people had not always had a flag of the United States. There had been a time when they had flown the flag of Spain and later on of Mexico. The first settlers of Santa María-of-the-Gardens had come from Spain through Mexico. They had come with their burros and carts up the Royal Road from Mexico. They had camped at the foot of the mountain. There they had built their church. There they had built their town.

All the people of the town always had lived in the town. That is, all but Pierre—"Old Frenchy," they called him—and Paco. Old Frenchy and Paco were newcomers. Everyone knew why they had come. Everyone knew Paco. Everyone knew him and loved him.

They did not know Old Frenchy very well. They knew that he had come from France. They thought that perhaps in his youth he had been one of the French trappers who had come down as far as Taos.

15

But whatever Old Frenchy had been as a young man, he was not a trapper now. He neither trapped nor hunted. He never came down into the town. Day after day, year after year, he spent his time carving little wooden figures. He carved all the animals and the birds of the mountains and the canyons. He knew them well. He must have loved them.

Paco knew the town. Once every month he would come down the mountain trail. He would walk along the crooked streets. As he passed by, he would look at the houses and the gardens. Sometimes he would touch the garden flowers. He never picked them.

When he reached the plaza he would sit by the well and look at the school and the children. Then he would go to the store to trade the wood carvings for coffee and salt and lard and cornmeal. When he had finished he would trudge up the mountain trail, not looking backward.

Through the years the people of the town watched for him. They were always surprised at his yellow hair and brown eyes, so unlike their black-eyed, black-haired children. They were always a little sad at his silent, serious ways so unlike their merry, noisy children. They grew to love him and to wait for his coming. They made excuses to pass him so they could say, "*Adíos,* Paco, *adíos.*"

But this morning no one passed him. It was too early.

16

The people were sleeping. The town and the houses were dark. The fires in the fireplaces had burned to ashes. There was no lamplight in any window, none excepting the window of the Padre's house. There a tiny light beckoned anyone who might be passing by.

Paco went to the Padre's door, but he did not knock. He felt shy and strange. He did not know the Padre, not well. He did not know any of these people of the town, not well. He had nodded to them only as they spoke to him as he passed by. What would he say to them? How would he speak to them? He knew Spanish, as he knew French. But words in any language came hard with him. He knew them, but to say them was more difficult. He was not used to talking, not to people.

As he waited, hesitating to knock, the Padre opened the door. "Good morning, Paco," the old priest said cheerfully. Then, almost as if he had expected the boy to come, he said, "So at last Old Frenchy needs help. Come in and rest. I will call the others."

PACO never could remember, afterwards, when the men came to the Padre's house. Suddenly they were there. There seemed to be so many of them. He had seen them before, all of them, many times. But he had never seen them together, crowded into one small room.

He tried to sort them out, as they stood talking together. There was the Padre, old and gentle, and the Alcalde, big and strong. The Alcalde's voice was big and strong, also. This was as it should be, Paco thought, for one who governed the people of the town.

The Maestro was tall and thin—a learned man, Pierre had said. He and the Padre spoke English as well as French and Spanish. French and Spanish were easy, Paco thought. English was the elegant language, one he would like to learn perhaps, sometime.

The Storekeeper and the Postmaster were brothers and looked and acted alike. They were short and fat and jolly. They made Paco feel happy to look at them.

Now they crowded the Padre's room. They talked

at the same time. They asked questions and answered their own questions.

"Is Old Frenchy sick?" the Storekeeper asked. "Of course he is sick," he answered himself. "Why else would he send for help?"

"Will he let us help him? Of course he will. That is why we go there," his brother, the Postmaster, asked and answered.

Paco felt confused. But he was relieved, too. He had been afraid that he would need to do all the talking. He was not used to talking, not much. There was so little that needed to be said to Pierre. The animals of the mountain top needed only a call or a whistle to know that he was nearby. There had been a time when he had tried talking with them. But they never answered. So he had stopped or almost stopped. Sometimes he talked a little, but not much.

Soon he found himself with the others going up the mountain trail. It was morning now. The sun was bright in the valley and bright on the mountain slope. The air was fresh and clean and sweet with the smell of pine and cedar.

The men talked and shouted. Stones rattled down the trail. Twigs snapped and branches bent. There was neither sight nor sound of animals. Only the birds safely overhead scolded the strangers who invaded their home.

Paco smiled to himself. He knew there were deer and grey squirrels, rabbits and chipmunks watching from hideouts. He wondered what they would do if he gave their call. Would they come to him? Would they run away, thinking he had betrayed them, keeping company with men?

After a while the group reached the clearing on the mountain top. The old man was lying as Paco had left him. He was lying in his blanket on the ground. His face was flushed. His eyes burned with fever. But he knew the men. He was glad to see them. He knew why they had come.

The men were quiet. They let the Padre do the talking for them.

"Monsieur, will you come with us?" the Padre asked. His voice was gentle and soft. His eyes were kind. The old man nodded.

"Will you let us send you to Santa Fe? The good Sisters there will take care of you. Soon you can be with us again. Will you go, Monsieur?" Again the old man nodded.

"I, myself, will take you," the Alcalde added. "I have two strong horses and a good wagon. It will be my pleasure, Monsieur, to take you and the boy."

At this the Old One became very excited. He tried to sit up. His voice rose shrilly. "No, no, not the boy. Paco must stay here. He is not old enough to go among strangers to lead them. He does not know enough—not yet—to teach them. The boy must stay here—in the mountains, near you. You are not strangers."

It was the men's turn to become excited. They waved their arms and shouted. "Not here alone in the mountains." "He is too young." "The winter is too long."

The thin tall Maestro leaned over the old man. "Not here. He belongs in my schoolroom. He is old enough to learn from books. I need him as a scholar."

The Storekeeper pushed him aside. "No, no," he shouted. "Let him make his home with me. I need him in my store." The fat Postmaster wrung his fat hands, crying, "No, no, no, no, I need him to carry letters. A postmaster should have a letter carrier."

The Padre made himself heard above the din. His soft voice was not gentle now. It was cold and firm. "Let there be silence," he told the men grouped about the sick one. "I am the Padre here. You, Monsieur, will go to the Sisters in Santa Fe until you are well again. Do you not agree? Is that not right? You, Paco, will live in town. When you feel the need you will return to the mountains to do that which Monsieur wants you to do. In the town you will have a good home. I myself will see to it. This is what will be. It is God's will I am sure of it."

Then, bending over the Old One, his voice became

gentle again. "Be at peace, Pierre. Your friends will carry you down the mountain. Young Paco and I will lead the way."

It was a strange procession down the mountain. The boy and the priest went first. The four men followed closely, carrying tenderly, safely, the sick one in his blanket.

They took him to the church where the Padre washed and blessed him. The brothers brought coffee and soup and the Maestro fed him. The Alcalde went to get his horses and his wagon.

Paco held the Old One's hand. He had never thought about loving the Old One. But now he knew he loved him. He knew he would miss him. He knew that he wanted him back when summer came again. Tears filled his eyes as he looked down at the sick old man. "Pierre," he said softly. The Old One told him, "I'll be back. Be a good boy. I'll be back."

The Alcalde came with his horses and wagon. He was the only one in Santa María-of-the-Gardens to have a driving team and also a wagon. He was proud of them. He hoped nothing would happen to them on the rough road to Santa Fe. It was a hard drive: two days to go, two days returning. Only in dry weather could the trip be made with speed and safety.

Word had traveled around the town of the unexpected happening. "Old Frenchy is ill. Ah, *pobrecito.*

God help him." "The Alcalde is taking him to the little Sisters at Santa Fe." "Ah, such a distance! Such a journey. But it is what should be done. God go with them."

The people gathered in the plaza whispering together. The brothers brought blankets from the store to make a bed for the Old One to lie on. The young men lifted Old Frenchy into the wagon. Paco climbed on the wagon wheel to say a last word. Should he tell the Old One, he wondered, about his fear that he could never make the wild creatures know what he wanted them to know? "Pierre," he said. "Pierre."

Gently the Padre lifted the young boy from the wagon wheel. The Alcalde spoke to his horses. He turned them. They went slowly across the plaza. They went slowly across the river and along the road to Santa Fe.

It was then that Paco saw the people of the town. All of them were there by the church door in the plaza. They had come to tell Paco, "Welcome. God bless you."

Paco saw their kind eyes, their smiling faces. Through his tears he smiled shyly back at them.

The Maestro and the Storekeeper and the Postmaster began talking again. "He is to go with me." "No, no, with me, with me." "But I need him." "Pardon, Señor, my need is greater."

The Padre looked at them. He looked at each one in

turn. At last they were quiet. They were good men, kind and good. Each man had wanted to be the one to give the boy a home. They had known him for so many years. They had watched him grow from baby-hood. They had worried about him, there on the moun-tain top with only Old Frenchy to care for him. Now they were silent. They waited for the Padre to speak. They waited for the Padre to choose the lucky one.

Then Tomás, one of the younger men, came to stand before the Padre. Lightly he touched young Paco's shoulder. "Let me have him, Father," he begged. "He needs what I can give him."

"Ah," the Padre said. "So . . . ?" He was smiling, looking at the young man. "You speak not of your need, but of his need. Talk frankly, Tomás. What is this he needs from you?"

"A home, Father, and love and laughter."

"A home, Tomás?" the Padre was teasing.

"I am building a house now, but soon—who knows?" Tomás was embarrassed. He stole a look at the pretty young woman standing behind Paco. She tossed her head. She would not look at him. The crowd laughed. "Who knows what can happen?" they teased Tomás.

The Padre looked at Paco. "And you," he asked the boy, "do you accept this that is offered you?"

"Yes, Father. Yes," Paco answered. His eyes were

26

shining through his tears. He looked at the young man standing beside him. "Yes, Señor Tomás, I thank you for your offer."

"Not Señor Tomás," the young man said. "Not Señor Tomás. To you it is Tío Tomás. I shall be your uncle. You are my family now."

Paco turned to hear soft laughter. The pretty, young woman standing behind him smiled mischievously. She whispered softly, so only the boy would hear. "Soon, I may be your Tía Pita. Who knows what can happen?"

The boy looked at her with wide eyes. He started to turn to Tío Tomás. The young woman shook her head. Her face was full of laughter. Her eyes were dancing with mischief. She put her finger to her lips and smiled and walked away. This was their secret. It was not to be shared. Not with anyone. Not even with Tío Tomás.

The Storekeeper shook Tomás' hand. "So you are the lucky one," he said. "You must be a good uncle, Tío Tomás, or you will have my anger heaped upon you."

The Postmaster, not to be outdone, put his arm across Tomás' shoulder. "Come, come. We must have a little fiesta to welcome Paco to our town."

The Maestro spoke quietly. "Remember, Tomás, I need him in my schoolroom."

Once again the Padre's voice was heard above the other voices. "We will have a little church-going before

27

we have the little fiesta," he told his people. "Come, Paco, I will show you how to pull the bell-rope for morning Mass."

The people laughed and moved into the church. Lightly they touched Paco as they passed him. They gave him little smiles and little teasing words. It was their welcome. They opened their hearts and their house doors to the boy from the mountain top.

PACO went home with Tío Tomás. He went home to the new house Tío Tomás was building. Two rooms were finished. One, the bedroom for Tío Tomás, had a small corner fireplace. The other room was the kitchen. It had a cooking fireplace, larger than the one used just for heating. It was a long room. It had to be long because it had so many uses. Here the food would be stored, and cooked and eaten. At one end was the workroom space. Here Tío Tomás would make what furniture was needed. The kitchen was large enough for sitting, too, when neighbors came for fiesta or for visiting.

Each room had an outside door and a window. There were no doors in the door frames. Not yet. There were no panes of glass in the windows. Tío Tomás said these would come later. "Now," he said, "we must build your room, Paco."

Paco could not believe that he was to have a room. A room in a house! A room that belonged to him!

Tío Tomás dug the trench for the foundation. Paco carried big stones from the riverbed to fill it in.

The boy had never known such happiness. The days were long and warm and golden with autumn sunshine. Even summer days on the mountain top had been cool with mountain winds and the snow that lay deep in the canyons. Even midday, there, had been darkened with the tall pines' shading. It had always been so quiet. Even the bird songs had a brooding stillness. But here in the little valley town it was filled with sounds of people talking, people calling to one another. It was filled with the sounds of laughter and of people singing.

At first the boy had worried about the Old One. Was he very ill? Would he get well again? Did he feel strange in the strange town of Santa Fe? Did he like the little Sisters? Were they giving him good care? Did he miss the mountain clearing that he knew as home? He worried about other things, too. What were the animals doing at home on the mountain? When he went back again would they have forgotten him?

He thought often of the day they had brought old Pierre down from the mountain and the Alcalde had taken him to Santa Fe. After they had gone, Pierre and the Alcalde, the days seemed very long. The nights seemed very lonely.

But on the evening of the fifth day the Alcalde came back along the road from Santa Fe. Long before the Alcalde's wagon reached the plaza, the people had

heard it coming. They came running from their houses and their gardens. They came running from their corn-fields on the mountain slope. They came running from the riverbank where they were washing clothes. Now they waited in the plaza. They waited for the Alcalde and his team and wagon.

Tío Tomás had been digging and Paco had been carrying stones when they heard the wagon. But now they, too, were in the plaza, waiting with the other people.

The wagon stopped in front of the church. The Al-calde sat in the high wagon seat, looking at the people. He was tired, but happy. Happy that he was home again. Happy that he had gone. At last he spoke, know-ing what the people wanted to hear.

"He is better," he told them. "Old Frenchy is going to get well. He likes his bed and his food. He likes the good care the little Sisters give him. He said," the Alcalde looked at Paco, "that now that he has thought about it, perhaps it is right that you live in the town. Perhaps it is God's will that your life becomes larger."

Paco nodded but he did not speak. He knew he must go back to the mountain. Some way he must know if the wild creatures loved him.

The people were glad to hear that Old Frenchy was getting better. They had many things to ask about Santa Fe, too. Only a few of the young men, like

Tomás, had ever been there. Only a few of the young men had gone beyond the valley of Santa María.

They asked the Alcalde questions. "Is it big, this town of Santa Fe?" "Is it very grand?" "Are all the people *rico* and elegant?"

The Alcalde answered every question. He answered with patience. He answered at length and in detail. He was their governor. It was his duty to lead them in their search for knowledge. He had much to tell them, of Santa Fe and of other places. As a young man, he had traveled widely, to Santa Fe, to Mora and down the Road through Santa Fe to Mexico.

Paco listened. The Old One had told him, a little, about the small French settlement in the valley beyond. He had told him, a little, of their home village in France. But those places seemed of the long-ago and not quite real. It was only two days ago that the Alcalde had been to Santa Fe.

So Paco listened, wanting to believe, not quite believing. He could not imagine a town more beautiful than Santa María-of-the-Gardens. He could not imagine a bigger town than this one with its plaza, church and store, and schoolhouse. He could not imagine streets more beautiful than these four streets bordered with flower gardens and paved with river stones.

He was glad that the Old One liked Santa Fe. The knowledge had taken a burden from his heart. As for himself, he was happy here in the town so near his mountain. But some day he must go back up to the mountain. He must go back to the wild creatures there. He must do what the Old One expected of him.

Each morning the boy was up before the sun. Each night he was asleep almost as soon as he had unrolled his blanket beneath the stars.

The new room went up quickly once they had started on its walls. He and Tío Tomás went to the sawmill up the canyon. They went for boards for the door and window frames. They went to a high mountain meadow to cut aspen poles for the *vigas*. They cut smaller slender aspen to make the ceiling above the *vigas*. They shoveled dirt on top to make the roof. They smoothed the dirt floor inside the room.

When they had finished the room, Tío Tomás decided to build a lean-to. "We will build it on the kitchen end of the house," he told Paco. "We will make the opening at the end away from the wind."

"But why a lean-to, Tío Tomás? We have our sleeping rooms. Why do we need a lean-to?"

Paco was remembering his lean-to on the mountain top. He wondered worriedly if, after all, his room was not for him. He wondered if Tío Tomás was building the lean-to for him, Paco. He hoped not. A lean-to was all right, but not as beautiful as a room.

Tío Tomás saw the boy's worried look. He knew

what Paco was thinking. "Don't worry, Paco," he laughed. "This lean-to is not for you. You have a room. This is for our animals."

"Our animals?" Paco asked in surprise. "But we haven't any animals."

Tomás laughed again. "We haven't any animals now, but some day we may have. We may have many things some day. Who knows? A month ago I did not have a young Paco to share my house with me. Who knows what we may have in another month?"

It was Paco's turn to laugh, but suddenly his laughter stopped in his throat. "I wish we had animals now," he said slowly. "I love animals. They are the big things I miss living here with you, my Tío Tomás. I had so many up yonder on the mountain. Rabbits and squirrels and deer, all kinds of animals."

"Would you like to have one of them down here?" Tomás asked. "We could trap one for you and build a cage for it until we had it tamed."

Paco was shocked. "No, no, no, no, Tío Tomás. They are free up there. They would not be happy here. They are wild. All but the dog, the wild dog."

"The wild dog?" Tío Tomás asked.

"He is wild now," Paco answered. "I don't think he always has been wild. I don't think he wants to be wild, but he can't help it."

Paco looked up at the mountain. Tears filled his eyes.

"If you want, we will go get him." Tío Tomás' voice was gentle.

Paco shook his head. "He would never come. All the animals came close to me, but never the wild dog. He would look at me, but he would not come close enough for me to pat him. I think he wanted to come, but he never did."

"Would you like me to get you a dog?" Tomás asked. "Now that we have a house, we need a dog. I would get one for you. He would be your dog."

Paco shook his head again. "The wild dog is my dog but he doesn't know it. But thank you, Tío Tomás."

Tomás turned away. His eyes smarted. Paco was so young, so independent. He was so grateful for every little thing, never forgetting to say thank you. Tomás wondered if the boy felt trapped down here in the valley. He wondered if he felt free.

He asked him, "Do you want to go back to your mountain top, Paco?"

"Yes, when we get our house built. I must go back. I have things to do there."

Tomás made his voice gruff so as not to show how he felt. "All right, Señor Paco, help me build this lean-to. After that there's a big thing I'll need your help with before you can go visit the squirrels and the rabbits."

Paco laughed. He forgot his moment of grieving. "What big thing, Tío?"

36

But Tomás would not tell him. "One thing at a time. For now it's getting this lean-to finished."

They could not build the lean-to with adobe. Tomás had used all the adobe bricks he had made when he built the extra room for Paco. "It takes a long time to make adobe. I'm in a hurry. I have to write a letter."

"A letter? To the Old One? About me?"

"No, Paco. Not to Old Frenchy. Not about you. You will know when the time is right."

That was all Tío Tomás would say.

The man and the boy went again to the high meadow to cut aspen poles. These they used to make the two walls and the slanting roof of the lean-to. They chinked the cracks between the poles with adobe mud. When they had finished, the lean-to was waterproof and windproof. It would shelter the animals, when they got them, from wind and sun and storm.

"It's a much better shelter than I had up on the mountain," Paco boasted.

"It's a good shelter. It goes with the house," Tomás said. He looked at Paco. "And now for the letter! We will ask the Maestro to help us. He knows about such things."

"Now? At once? Tonight?" Paco asked.

"No. Not tonight. Tomorrow. Early in the morning. Tonight I will sit and think about the letter. Tonight I can sit and dream."

Far into the night Tío Tomás sat outside the new-made shelter. He sat looking at the stars and dreaming dreams.

Paco lay on his blanket and looked at the stars. But he was not dreaming dreams or thinking thoughts. He was too sleepy.

THE next day was full of surprises. From sun-up in the morning until the stars were dim in the late night sky there were surprises and surprises and surprises.

The day did not begin as if it were an important day. Tío Tomás was unusually quiet. He did not make jokes as he did every other morning. He did not say teasing things to show Paco how much he liked him. He did not laugh. His black eyes did not even smile. His face was tight and closed looking.

Then, too, he acted strangely. He burned the tortillas on the tin top of the campfire in the yard. He spilled the coffee. He did not eat his breakfast.

Paco was worried. He smiled at his Tío Tomás. He began to talk to him. "I thought perhaps, now that our house is finished, we would eat in the kitchen."

"It isn't finished," Tomás told him. "Only my work is finished."

Paco did not know what else to say. He ate his breakfast in silence. When he had finished, Tomás spoke to

39

him, kindly. "Come, we will go to my sister's house, where my father lives. I have things to ask him."

Paco was pleased. He liked Tomás' older sister. Tía Carmen, he called her. He liked her husband. He liked Tomás' father, an old, old man. He was even older, Paco thought, than Pierre, his own Old One.

When they reached Tía Carmen's house, Tomás greeted his father and his sister and Carlos, her husband. They spoke of the corn harvest and the apricots that grew wild by the river. They spoke of the new house and how, come spring, the church would need new whitewash.

Even Paco knew that what they talked about was not what his Tío had come to talk about. But this was the Spanish way. It was the polite way. One approached slowly and with dignity. One never rushed.

Paco began to think of other things. He thought about his room and wondered when he could sleep there. He thought about the letter Tomás would write and wondered about it. Suddenly he realized that polite talk had stopped. Tomás was saying what he had come to say.

Paco could not believe his ears when he heard what it was. Tomás was asking his father's permission to marry. Paco had thought that Tío Tomás would never need to ask anyone for anything. Besides, he was asking to marry. Paco was not certain that he, Paco, was pleased about this. Who was she, he wondered.

"Who is the Señorita?" the father asked gravely. Paco thought he saw a twinkle in the old man's eyes. Tía Carmen also was smiling. "They know," Paco said to himself. Suddenly he remembered Señorita Pita and the secret that they shared. If it was Señorita Pita it would be all right, he thought, and listened for the answer.

"Señorita María Dolores Guadalupe Chacon," Tomás answered proudly.

"Ah! María Pita," the old man said. "Pita," Carmen nodded to her husband. "The Señorita!" Paco smiled. Everything was fine. It would be fun having a Tía Pita.

The older people were talking. "She is beautiful and good," Tomás said. "She can cook and sew," Carmen added. "She goes to Mass on Sunday," the old man spoke thoughtfully. After a time he said, "Yes. It is agreed. Señorita María Dolores Guadalupe Chacon will make a good wife for you, my son."

They went to the Padre's house to ask his blessing. "What a surprise, a surprise!" the Padre kept repeating. Paco knew he was teasing. Then he went with the family to the house of the Maestro. They needed the Maestro to help write the letter. The letter was important. It would ask the parents of María Pita and her

41

grandfather and her uncles if they would permit Tomás to ask the beautiful Pita to marry him.

Paco laughed. To think that Tío Tomás would need
to ask. Everyone was shocked. "This is serious," Carmen said. "It is our custom," the old man spoke sternly.

The Maestro was cross. "This is not for laughter," he
told Paco. "If the family accepts him, they will give
him a fiesta to show approval. If they do not accept
him, they will send him a squash. Do you think a
squash would be something to laugh at?"

"Not to accept him? Give him a squash?" Paco asked
in horror.

"A squash," the Maestro answered. "It will be too
bad for your uncle if the family of Pita hands him the
squash." Paco had no answer. He was too worried.

It took almost all morning to make the letter, to find
the right words, to write them elegantly enough to be
certain to please the family of Pita. At last it was finished to everyone's satisfaction. Then the Padre and
Tomás' father, the Maestro and Carmen's husband de-
livered it by hand to the house of Señor Chacon.

Paco and Tío Tomás went to their own house. Paco
was tired. It had been hard work to help write such an
important letter. He was worried, too. What if they
sent them a squash?

He stole a look at Tío Tomás. "We will sit in the
shade of our house and rest," he told his uncle. "We

will not even think. We have done enough thinking for today."

But when they reached their house another surprise was awaiting them.

The yard and the house were filled with all the older women of Santa María. They were inside the house and outside and on the roof. The yard was filled with buckets of water they had carried from the river. There were sacks of clay they had carried up from the clay pit. There were baskets of gypsum they had dug from a cliff cave in the lower canyon.

They had brought a hollow log. Here they were mixing the clay to plaster smoothness and thickness. They were mixing it with their bare feet.

They had brought their wooden paddles and their wooden trowels. They had brought their plastering mittens made of rabbit fur. They had brought noise and talk and laughter and gaiety

They were having a wonderful time.

They told Tomás and Paco to go away some place. They had come to plaster the house inside and outside. This was woman's work, they said. They did not want men around.

"Come back at sunset time," they called after them. The man and the boy did not know what to do. They walked up and down the four short streets. The streets were dusty and empty.

They went into the church where Tomás lighted a candle before the Santa María. Paco knelt beside his uncle.

Then they wandered down to the riverbank and sat on the rocks and watched the trickle of water flow by. Paco threw stones and thought about squashes. Tomás sat. Perhaps he was thinking, too.

At sunset time they went home, thinking the day was almost over. Paco gasped in delight at what he saw. Outside, the house walls were smooth and golden coffee-brown in color. In the smoothness of the plaster he could see the patting of many mittened hands. Even the dirt roof had been wet down with pails of river water. Everything was damp and fresh and clean and smelled earth-wet and sun-warmed.

Paco wanted to run inside to see his room. Politeness forced him to walk as slowly as Tomás walked.

They went first into the kitchen room. The fireplace and knee-high border around the walls had been plastered with gold-yellow clay flecked with mica. "Fool's gold," mica was called, and though it was not gold it was as pretty. Above the border of fool's gold the walls were dazzling white with gypsum. The window frame and door frame had been painted blue with store paint. They were the same color blue as all the other windows and doors in Santa María-of-the-Gardens. "Blessed Virgin Blue," the people called it. They used it to honor the *patrona* of their town.

44

The dirt floor of the kitchen had been plastered and hand-patted smooth like the outside walls. Then it had been polished with rubbing stones until it was a glistening hardness.

They went into Tomás' room and at last into Paco's. These rooms were the same. They had been done in the same way, using the same materials and the same colors.

"But mine is the most beautiful," Paco thought. "It is the most beautiful room in all the world."

When they went outdoors again, Tomás made a speech of thank-you to the women. He spoke with gratitude and dignity. It was a lovely speech. It made the women cry.

Then it was Paco's turn. He stood straight like Tomás had stood. He made a little bow with his hand on his heart as Tomás had done. But when he tried to talk, he had nothing to say. All that he could think of was, "Thank you. Thank you very much."

Now that the women had finished, they sat on the ground outside the house. They were very quiet. They were very tired. Peace and contentment sat with them. Memories sat with them, memories of their houses when they were young.

The sunset sky still lingered red and gold. The church bell rang its evening blessing for the people of the valley. The younger women and the girls of the town came singing down the crooked street. In their

hands were pails and kettles. On their heads were cloth-tied bundles. They were bringing fiesta supper for all the people of the town.

The campfire in the yard was lighted. Soon the evening air was filled with the smells of burning cedar, of bubbling stew and fresh boiled coffee.

Then the men came and the children. The men brought gifts for the new house. They brought panes of glass for the windows and pairs of hinges for all the doors. They brought two benches and three handmade chairs.

The brothers came, the Storekeeper and the Postmaster. They brought a narrow, hand-carved bed. "This is for Paco," they said. "It would have been his, if he had lived at our house."

The Alcalde came. He brought a hand-carved chest. "Paco's chest," he said, putting it in Paco's room.

The Maestro came. He brought a slate and a slate pencil. "For school," he said, looking sternly at Paco.

All the children ran shouting through the rooms. Their gift was young-hearted, light-hearted laughter.

The Padre came to bless the house and hang a crucifix above the door.

Supper was served and the good food was eaten. The men sat outside in the evening light. Someone strummed a guitar and the young men sang. The young women sat in the kitchen with their mamas, their grandmamas, and their aunts.

Paco peeked in. He was looking for the beautiful Pita. He saw her, sitting quietly between her mother and her grandmother. Her hands were folded in her lap. Her eyes were downcast. She was neither talking, nor listening to the others talk. Paco looked at her. He wanted to say something, but, of course, no boy ever spoke to a Señorita when she was with her mother.

Suddenly Pita looked up. She looked at Paco, her face full of mischief, her black eyes shining. She smiled and put a finger to her lips. She shrugged a shoulder. Her mother turned. Her grandmother turned. They looked at the girl who sat between them. Pita did not see them. Her eyes were looking down. Her hands were folded in her lap.

But Paco knew something. There would be no squash.

A WEEK went by slowly, slowly, slowly.

"A day at a time makes the year go by," Tío Tomás would say every evening. He would look up the crooked street as he said it.

Then at last the morning came when his letter was answered. The Padre and Señor Chacon and his brothers and his oldest son came to Tomás' house. They came to ask Tomás and all his relatives to a *prendorio*.

To be asked to such a fiesta meant that the family of Pita had accepted Tomás. It meant, also, that the Señorita Pita would most probably accept him.

The *prendorio* would be held in two days. There were many things Tomás had to do. But all his family helped him. His father and the husband of Carmen brought him an old carved chest.

"I gave this to your mother at her *prendorio*," the old man said proudly, "as my father before me gave it to his bride at her *prendorio*. Look in it, Son. These are the things that have been handed down from mother to son for at least two hundred years. They are what we brought with us from Spain."

49

Paco helped Tomás unpack the chest. There was a silk embroidered shawl, a lace mantilla as fine as a spiderweb. There was a yellowed ivory fan, and a high gold comb for the hair. These were the things from Spain. They were very old and very precious.

There were also things brought many years ago from Mexico. There was a silver necklace, and a pair of earrings. There was a gold filigree locket on a slender chain.

Tomás looked at the chest. The things it held had value because they were the symbols of what had lasted. Other things must go into the chest also. They were the things that he would put in. It was Spanish custom that he buy dresses and shoes for the first year of his wife's marriage and ornaments that would last her lifetime and afterwards.

All the family went with Tomás to the store on the plaza. They went with him to watch him, to advise him and to enjoy this important occasion. It took a long time. There were many things to be bought and each one must be chosen with care and good taste. The last thing Tomás bought was a great black shawl with wide black fringe. When a Señorita became a bride it was proper that she own a black, fringed shawl to wear to Mass on Sundays.

At last the chest was packed. The lid was closed, not to be opened by Tomás again.

50

The night of the *prendorio* came at last. Everyone went to the house of Señor Chacon. Everyone in the town went because everyone was related to someone who was related to Pita or to Tomás. They sat in the parlor and talked of crops and weather and the coming winter.

After a while Tomás' father stood up. He made a fine speech and a long one with many words, as it should be. At the end he asked Señor Chacon to bring in his beautiful daughter so that the family of Tomás could meet her. Everyone kenw her. They had seen her every day of her life. But this was not important. It was Spanish custom to ask to meet her. It was Spanish custom that her father bring her into the parlor and present her to the father of the young man who wanted to marry her.

Gravely the beautiful Pita took the old man's arm. Gravely they walked around the room. Her voice was low as she greeted her new family. Her eyes were downcast. She looked at no one until she came to Paco. Quickly she flashed him a look full of fun and mischief. "What did I tell you?" her black eyes said. Then gravely she went around the circle.

She was presented with the chest and the treasures in it. This she accepted with courtesy and pleasure. Then she gave Tomás a rosary. This, too, was custom.

Many speeches were made. Carlos, Carmen's husband, had made a poem. He recited it to the people. There was guitar playing and singing. There was hot chocolate thickened with egg whites to drink. There were many kinds of sweet cakes to eat.

It was a wonderful party. But at last it was over. Everyone went home. They went home happy. It had been a good *prendorio*. Pita had accepted Tomás. They would be married. The wedding day had been chosen.

Paco never knew how much time had passed between the *prendorio* and the wedding day. There had been so many things to do. There had been so many people around. There was so much joyful giving and gay teasing and happy confusion.

The Postmaster and the Storekeeper were chosen as the *padrinos* and their wives were the *madrinas*. This meant a fiesta at their houses with music and dancing and all kinds of refreshments. This meant, too, that they bring gifts to the new household. They brought a store-bought bed and a homemade cornhusk mattress. They brought three pillows stuffed with feathers.

Pita's mama and her aunts and her sisters came also to the new house. They brought Pita's dishes that her father had bought in Santa Fe. They brought silver knives and spoons that had belonged to Pita's grandmother. They brought three copper kettles and two woolen blankets and geraniums in bright tin cans.

52

They hung curtains at the windows and put Indian blankets on the floor.

Pita did not come with them. It would have been improper for her to come. "But she told us what to bring and where to put them," her younger sister said to Paco when her mother could not hear her.

The morning of the wedding came. Bright and early all the people of the town went to stand in little groups before the house of María Dolores Guadalupe Chacon.

Everyone had on Sunday clothes. Paco had new blue trousers and a new red shirt. He wore shoes instead of sandals. Tomás had on the suit he had bought when he worked in Santa Fe. Everyone looked elegant.

Pita came out of the house, her small hand resting on her father's arm. She was a picture no one would ever forget. She wore the white dress Tomás had bought for her. She wore the Spanish shawl and the lace mantilla and the high gold comb that had been in the carved chest. She wore the filigree necklace that brides of Tomás' family had worn on their wedding days.

Two young men who played guitars and the old blind fiddler led the procession. The people formed in line. They knew their places. Custom, as old almost as the hills around them, had made a pattern which they did not change.

53

Paco walked with the father of Tío Tomás. He felt
solemn and proud to be walking there. He was one of
the family.

The church bell rang and the procession moved forward to the music of guitar and violin. The Padre said
the Mass. He married María Dolores Guadalupe to the
proud and happy Tomás. He blessed them. He blessed
the people.

The wedding Mass was over. The church bells rang.
The young men shot their guns. Powder smoke mingled with the smell of incense and with candle wax
inside the church. It mingled with the smell of autumn
flowers in the gardens of the town and with cedar and
piñon on the mountain slopes.

The Padre led the procession now. He walked behind the musicians. Tomás and his bride were first in
the line that followed him. They walked across the
plaza. They walked down the crooked street. They
walked to the new house that stood waiting for them.

Pita and Tomás walked through the door together.
But once inside they stopped. They turned around.
They beckoned Paco. Each one gave him a hand. They
led him into his new home.

"Your house, Paco," Tomás said.

"Your home, Paco," Pita whispered. "Your home,
your Tío Tomás, and your Tía Pita."

56

PACO stretched sleepily. He did not want to waken. Not yet. He was too sleepy and too comfortable. He stretched again and turned over, pushed his face into a pillow. He pushed his face deep into it. Its softness surprised him. It was fluffy and fat. It smelled clean.

The boy raised his head. He opened sleep-heavy eyes and squinted down at the pillow. This was a real pillow, not a rolled-up piece of blanket. A real pillow! He turned on his side for better seeing. He was in a bed. A real bed!

Still half asleep, he sat up and looked around. He saw a small room with whitewashed walls and a knee-high border of yellow clay. The bright blue door was closed. The deep-set square of window had pink curtains, and peeking between them was a red blossoming geranium in a bright tin can. The standing-up pieces of cedar-wood kindling in the corner fireplace were ready for the morning fire. Above the fireplace a blue and gold picture of the Santa María smiled down at him.

57

Paco rubbed his eyes, sleepily trying to think. Where was he? He could not remember. None of this could be real. It could not be true. This was not the place where he had lived for always.

This could not be his bed. He was not used to a bed like this one. His bed had been a blanket on the ground.

This room could not be his room. He was not used to a room in a house. His room had been a lean-to shelter built against a tall pine tree. There were no windows, only cracks. There was no door, only an opening, blanket-covered.

None of this was true, the boy decided. It could not be real, but it was nice. It was beautiful and wonderful. It was comfortable and good. Carefully he lay down again. He put his head back on the soft, clean pillow. He pulled up the soft, clean blanket and tucked it beneath his chin. Under him, the cornhusk mattress made friendly, crackling noises when he moved. Quickly, tightly, he shut his eyes.

If this was a dream, he would go back to sleep and dream again.

Almost at once, he was asleep. Almost at once, he was deep in a dream. But he did not dream of the wonderful room. He dreamed of the things he had known for always. He dreamed of Pierre, the Old One he had lived with on top of the mountain. The Old One was a silent and serious man. He talked little. He never sang. He never laughed. But all day long he carved little wooden animals. He carved them with love and understanding. He carved them true to life and full of the joy of living. It was as if he were trying to make amends for having once trapped and killed them. But he never talked about them. When he talked, it was about the French settlement and the people who had lived there. It was about his dream of leading men into a gentle way of life. He talked with words only, never in sentences. Paco never understood all that the Old One tried to tell him.

What the Old One wanted was for the boy to learn to live in peace with all God's creatures, to follow in the footsteps of Saint Francis. Paco knew that the Old One wanted him to be like the Saint. But Saint Francis had talked with the birds and tamed the wolves and given sermons that were understood by the animals of the mountain top. Paco had never found any sign that the wild ones loved him or understood him.

One thing he knew. He knew it without words. The Old One liked him. He liked it when the wild things of the mountains came to him. He liked it that all wild things seemed to trust him. He liked it that he, Paco, did not know the meaning of fear.

But the Old One's approval was silent approval. He never said it with words.

The mountain clearing where they lived was never filled with laughter nor with talking. But it was not a sad place. The boy thought of it as right and good. He had learned to hear the many little noises, each one big in its own importance because it told of the life that filled the mountains and the canyons.

The boy dreamed of these things now.

He heard again all the early morning sounds that had wakened him each day as long as he could remember. He heard again, in his dream, the soft morning prayer-song of the mountain birds. He heard the feathered rustle of their night-rested wings.

He heard the day wind in the treetop whispering to the cliffs of the canyon. He heard the tall pines murmuring to other trees. He heard the noisy mountain river scolding the small stones in its shallow bed. He heard the stones talking back to the river as its water pushed them and shoved them.

In his dreaming, a beaver slapped his broad flat tail on the river surface, giving his danger call. A grey squirrel dropped from the pine branch to the top of the lean-to shelter. A deer, on the edge of the clearing, flashed through the early sunlight and vanished in the underbrush.

The boy smiled in his sleep. These were the sounds that were good. These were the sounds that he knew.

Slowly day came to the town outside his window. Day came to Santa María-of-the-Gardens.

The sun peeped over the mountain. It moved down the mountain trail. It filled the dusty, crooked streets. It painted the windows of the houses with morning gold. It lighted the bell tower on the Church of Santa María.

One by one the blue doors opened in all the 'dobe houses. Smoke curled upward from all the breakfast fires. There was laughter at the well in the center of the plaza. There the big girls went for the day's supply of water. There they exchanged their secrets. Their voices and their laughter filled the bright, new day with bright, new sound.

The Alcalde's rooster crowed. The Maestro's brown dog barked. The Padre pulled the bell rope. The church bell rang its morning call.

Tía Pita, in her kitchen, began to sing.

"Pobrecito, Pobrecito,
You are sleeping.
Too long you are sleeping.
Daylight is creeping.
Too fast it is creeping.
Paco, Pobrecito,
Why don't you wake up?"

61

Paco came awake, wide awake. He knew where he was. He knew why he was here. All of this was real. He remembered. This was home.

Quickly he rolled out of bed. Quickly he dressed himself. This was his room, his house, his family. He felt bursting with happiness. Just as soon as he went into the kitchen, he would make up a song for Tía Pita and he would sing it to her. For many days, ever since the wedding, he and Tía Pita had been singing to each other. They made up their songs as they sang them. Tío Tomás laughed at them. They laughed, too. It was fun.

Paco opened his bright blue door. The mountain looked down at him. The boy stopped. He remembered his dream. He saw again the blue winged bluejay. He heard again the fretful cawing of the crows. He smelled the piñons and the cedar. He felt against his face the morning mist of the mountains. His breath caught in his throat. Longing choked him. He was homesick, homesick for the mountain clearing, for the mountain shelter, for the Old One and the campfire. He was homesick for the birds and the wild things of the mountain and the canyons. They were his friends. Were the mountain birds waiting for him? What did the wild ones think? Did they think he had left them, never to return?

Slowly he walked through the door and closed it after him. Slowly he walked along the sun-filled portal and into the kitchen. Tío Tomás was going to the yard for wood. He smiled at the boy. He pulled his hair. "Good morning, Señor Paco," he greeted him, teasing him, showing how much he liked him. Tío Tomás went outside, whistling his happiness.

Tía Pita looked at Paco. Her song had stopped. She was not smiling. There was no twinkle in her eyes. There was no mischief in her face. It was still and gentle. She had seen this coming. Often she had seen the boy looking up at the mountain. Loving his new home, perhaps he had not known that the mountain top was calling. But she had known. She had known that some day he would hear its call.

She spoke to the boy. "I know," she said softly. "I understand."

"You know?" Paco asked in wonder. "You know that I must go back? How could you know, Tía? I, myself, knew only a minute ago."

"My heart understands you," Pita answered.

The young woman led the younger boy to the doorway. She pointed to the mountain that towered above the town. "You are valley born, my Paco, but you are mountain bred. The mountain owns a part of you. It always will. It will call you, and when it does you must answer the call."

Pita pointed to the mountain trail that led upward from the crooked street. "There is the mountain trail, my Paco. Today it calls you. But remember, it is not

63

a going-away trail. It is not a trail that you walk but once. It is a pathway between homes—your clearing on top of the mountain, your house in the valley."

Tía Pita smiled at Paco and he smiled back at her. Kindness he had known, and approval. But understanding was new to him. Being able to talk about things was new to him. It was good. He felt happiness within him. Everything was all right. His wanting to go and his going was all right. If he ever felt the need to come back again, he would be welcome. He knew this.

Tío Tomás came in with an armful of wood. They sat down to breakfast. It was a merry meal. Tía Pita made it so.

"Young Paco is going back to his mountain today," she said. She spoke as if all of them had known that he would go, sometime. She spoke as if it was the right thing for him to do. She spoke as if, of course, Tomás would accept it.

Tomás looked sharply at his young wife. He was not sure that her light words came straight from a light heart. He thought he heard the sound of crying that her gay voice tried to hide. But whatever Pita wanted or Pita did would be right. He was sure of this.

So he smiled and nodded. "Of course you may go, but hurry back. The day will be a long one without you."

64

"A day?" Paco was troubled. "Not just a day, Tío Tomás. A year, I think." Then quickly, seeing sadness in the faces of the two he loved, he added, "Maybe not a year, Tío. As soon as I can I will come back again."

"We will be waiting, Paco," Tía Pita said. "Come now. You get your bedroll ready and I will prepare food for you to take with you."

Before the sun had finished its first hour across the day path in the sky, Paco was climbing the mountain trail.

Pita and Tomás watched him go. "The mountain is so big and he is so little," Pita said wiping her eyes. "He is so young and independent," Tomás added and, turning to look at his young wife, asked, "Will he come back?" Pita had gone into the kitchen. Tomás thought he heard her answer, "Who is there to know? Perhaps."

Tomás looked again at the mountain trail, but the trees seemed to be hiding the boy who walked beneath them. He looked again at the mountain. It stood brooding and dark, towering above the town.

To Paco, standing beside Tía Pita at the kitchen door, the mountain suddenly had looked dark and stern and unfriendly. Now that he was used to sunlight and singing, to talk and laughter, to family and neighbors, he almost had decided not to come. He knew the mountain and all the things it held. He knew the heaviness of its silence. He knew the loneliness of its solitude. For a second's breath, he almost turned away.

But the mountain called him. It demanded that he come. He had to go.

Now on the trail the town and the things of the town lay behind him. The mountain was not dark and stern. It was not unfriendly. It was a lovely world. Paco looked around him in delight.

The mountain slope was filled with early morning. The air sparkled. Sunbeams danced. Above him sheer rock cliffs glistened in pink mist. At his feet the sides of the trail were thick with flowers, sunflowers, margaritas, asters. On the lower slopes chamiso bushes

67

flamed in yellow. On the higher slopes the aspen quivered with gold. The ground oak was turning bronze. The kinni-kinnick berries were little and white, but after the first snow they would turn to crimson.

A deer leaped lightly across the trail. For a heartbeat's time they looked at each other. Paco wanted to leap, too, and bound into the underbrush. Being mountain bred, he knew that this was not the way. He walked on slowly, steadily. A bluejay scolded him. A chipmunk stopped to look at him.

In a short while he reached the first mountain meadow. It was green with thick grass, and flowers dotted it as stars dot the sky at night. Paco sat beside a trickle of river running through the tall grass. He washed his hot face. He took off his shoes and put his bare feet in the cold water.

This was what he wanted. This was where he belonged. He would never leave it again. He would never go back to the valley. He would stay forever deep in his mountain world.

Perhaps he slept a while. He did not know. He had no dreams to show him, only a quiet feeling to tell him that he was rested, that he must go on.

By mid-morning he had reached the clearing. It had a desolate, deserted look. It was cluttered with things that seemed out of place now that no one had been there to use them. At first glance he turned away. In

this small clearing fringed by tall pine trees there was neither order nor cleanliness in the man-made campsite.

He stood in the opening of his lean-to. It had been his shelter, a little warmer and a little drier than outside. This had been all that he expected or wanted then. When he had lived here, he had not thought about cleanliness nor comfort. But he thought about them now as he looked inside his shelter.

Pack rats had been everywhere. What they had taken he did not know, but what they had left in exchange was everywhere, bits of broken glass, a colored rock, a pine cone, a bunch of dried moss. Paco laughed softly to himself. He knew where the pack rats' nests were. There were many around the clearing. They were not afraid of him. Season after season they had played with him their game of give-and-take.

Paco threw his bedroll on the ground outside the shelter. After he had eaten he would clean the place. He would clean the Old One's shelter too, get it ready for the old man's return.

The boy stood in the clearing. It was so quiet, he could almost feel the silence. "I'm hungry," he said aloud, and the sound rippled the quiet like a stone thrown into still water.

He went to the river edge to eat his lunch. No wonder his packsack had been so heavy, he thought, as he opened it and looked inside. Tía Pita had given him many more things than salt and coffee, lard and cornmeal. There was green corn and chili and bean paste and chokecherry jam. There were tortillas wrapped in cornhusks ready for eating.

Paco was hungry. He had not known how hungry he was. He had not remembered what good food Tía Pita cooked. He thought of Tía Pita and how she was forever making soups and good things for him and Tío Tomás to eat. He thought of Tío Tomás and his friendly, teasing ways.

A camp-robber bird flew to his shoulder, hopped to his wrist and stole his tortilla right out of his hand. Then he flew away to eat his stolen prize. Paco shouted in delight, and all the birds in the bushes and treetops scolded him for such unseemly noise.

Suddenly the place was full of wild things. Long-tailed lizards sunned themselves on the river bank. Grey squirrels threw pine cones from the tree branches. Chipmunks fought over the bits of tortilla Paco threw to them. Water ouzels bobbed and danced on the rocks in the river. Bluejays chased away the smaller birds. A mountain trout shot upward like a silver arrow and down again into its still pool under the rock ledge.

Paco felt as if he never had been away. This was home. For a long time he sat watching the wild creatures about him. They looked at him with curious eyes.

71

After a while the boy left the river bank and went back to the clearing. It looked better at this second visit, not so forlorn, not so neglected. There was nothing here that he could not put right again. Quickly, with a singing heart, he began to work.

He hung his food supply away from the pack rats and the squirrels, the chipmunks and the brown bear. He undid his bedroll and put his blanket to sun. He cleaned the shelters, his lean-to and the Old One's, and cut pine branches for his blanket bed. He scoured the rusty axe blade and he cut the wood supply for the evening fire. He scooped out the blackened rain-soaked ashes from the unused campfire. He cleaned the coffee pot and frying pan with river sand and washed the gourd bowls with river water. He cleaned the spring of watercress and water bugs and spider webs and silted sand and filled the clay *tinaja* with cold spring water. He brushed the clearing with a pine-branch broom and built the supper fire.

After a while he finished. The clearing was in order. Everything was as it should be. The shelters smelled fresh and clean.

The afternoon had been a busy and a short one. Now evening shadows came swiftly. Night wind from the snow peaks brought its breath of cold. The wild things went away.

Night quiet filled the clearing.

Then Paco saw the wild dog. The wild dog was part of the shadow, part of the night wind and the night mist. For several years he had come, always at the same time of evening, hiding in the gathering darkness, watching, watching the boy but never coming to him. Tonight, like the many other nights, Paco whistled softly. He called gently, he threw bits of tortilla, he waited, but the wild dog would not come.

All at once Paco felt restless. The night was too still, too dark, the clearing too small with the tall trees pressing against it. The boy walked down the trail where it turned sharply and looked down upon a mountain meadow.

Night darkness had not filled the meadow. It was flooded in moonlight and silver mist. Even the shadows were streaked with silver and the tall grass was silver-tasseled. Paco had never seen it more beautiful nor peaceful. He lay on a rock ledge looking in wonder at the meadow beneath him.

As if they had been waiting for him, the jack rabbits came. They came in twos and threes, hopping and frisking in the pale moonlight. They made a sort of circle and played leapfrog and tag and catch-me-if-you-can. They played and played, and slowly the moon moved across the night sky.

Paco never knew how long he watched them, but all at once he was sleepy. He was very sleepy. He stumbled up the dark trail to the clearing, to his shelter and to sleep.

It had been a long, full day. It had been a busy, tiring day. He was too tired for dreaming. Far in the canyon below, the coyotes sang their nighttime concert.

Stealthily, slowly, not making a sound, not moving the bushes, not cracking a dry twig, the wild dog crept to the lean-to opening. He lay before the door, guarding the boy he wanted for master.

Night damp seeped into the shelter. Night winds moaned. Night hours passed.

The grey of before-dawn and morning mist moved into the clearing. Wild Dog went away.

The boy shivered, ending sleep. His teeth chattered. His breath made a smoke path in the frosty air. His hands and feet were almost too cold to move, but he moved them. He rolled from his blanket, chilled and stiff. Then, hurrying, he made the morning fire.

Once he got it started, its bright heat warmed him. Its bright blaze cheered him. Coffee and tortillas made him feel brave and strong. The long day stretched before him with its promise of adventure.

While he ate, banked the breakfast fire and put the camp in order, he planned his day. He would follow the river to its source and check the beaver dams along the way.

Going upstream was easy walking. He jumped from

rock to rock and whistled at the black crows. After a time the way grew narrower and steeper and the sun grew warmer. The boy rested often, watching the wild things about him at work and play.

The beavers had been busy in the time he had been gone. He found a new dam that they had built and a new beaver family.

The sun was at midday when Paco reached the river source. High in the cliff-face overhead, spring water leaped in a slender lacy waterfall to a rock cupped pool, cold and deep and still, a hundred feet below.

Paco had been here many times before. He loved the place. He climbed into the room behind the falls. Foam-tipped water spray flicked him gently, not wetting him, just touching him with fingertips of coolness. The walls of the room were of rock. Walls and ceiling and floor were covered with thick velvet moss. The green pool lay beneath him. The boy lay flat on the rock, hanging over, to look deep into its mystery that held the secrets of the centuries.

Then he went swimming, splashing and tumbling, diving deep and coming up for air. The water was icy cold. The air had grown colder, too, with a hint of snow. It was time for snow. It always came with the first of autumn. Even down in the valley there might be snow before the month was ended.

Paco dressed quickly. He did not want to be on the

75

cliff when snow came. He must hurry back to the clearing. He decided to take a short cut through the canyon below and then up onto the trail again.

He had gone but a short distance when he discovered the tracks. They were bear tracks—grizzly tracks perhaps, they were so large. A bear cub, maybe two, were with the larger bear. Paco remembered now. He had seen bear tracks yesterday, not far from the trail, close to the wild honeybee tree. He had intended to go back and track them, but he had forgotten in the work of cleaning the campsite.

He went slowly, cautiously, watching each step, making no sound whatever. Then he saw them, deep in the canyon below, a mother grizzly and two half-grown cubs. Paco tested the wind with a wet finger. He must stay against the wind. His scent must not be borne to the keen nostrils of the mother bear. There lay his safety. The grizzly, he knew, was afraid of only two things. The smell of smoke and the smell of man would send it into a frightened rage.

He was lucky. The wind was right for him. Unless it changed, the bears would never know an enemy was near.

Paco stopped to watch them. He knew that he should go on. He knew that snow was coming, but he had to watch. The mother bear and her cubs were playing. They were sliding down a slanted rock to the floor of the canyon. There they would box each other and

push and tumble. Then they would climb to the rock top to slide down again.

Paco chuckled. He had forgotten that there is reason for silent living on the mountain top. The mother bear paused in her play. She stood up on her hind legs and sniffed the air. She was a giant in size, four hundred pounds at least, thick-shouldered and silver-tipped.

Stiffly she began to lumber up the canyon side, straight in a line with Paco. The boy froze. He seemed to melt into the rock wall behind him. Halfway up the cliff, the mother bear stopped. She cuffed her cubs and sent them tumbling downward. Then, dropping to all fours, she followed them. Slowly, deliberately they crossed the canyon and climbed the other side.

It took a long time—almost as long, Paco thought afterwards, as it did for him to reach the clearing. Wild Dog was waiting for him, hiding in the shadows, patient and watchful. Paco called to him. He whistled. He got food out and threw him bits of it. Then he coaxed him, "Come, Wild Dog. I will be good to you. You were not always wild. I know you were not. Once you had a home and master."

The wild dog did not move. He only watched. "Look, Wild Dog," Paco pleaded, "you and I are the only one-things up here. All the other things go together. Bears with bears and deer with deer. You and I need each other."

78

The wild dog moved away. Paco neither saw nor heard him. He knew only that the dog had gone.

The boy turned blindly. He said aloud, not caring what wild thing heard him, "I'm going to look at the house in the valley. I won't go in or stay, but I will go close enough to look at it."

The trail was dark. Night comes quickly in the high places. Paco did not need light to see where he was going. He knew the trail. He knew every rock and every curve along its way. But it took time. The trail was steep. He had to feel his way with his footsteps.

At last he came above the town. Dimly he could make out the plaza of Santa María-of-the-Gardens. He could see the tiny finger of light in the Padre's window.

He could not see his house. He had to go down, down the slope before he could see it. It was dark like all the other houses. He looked again. There seemed to be a light. He went to the foot of the trail. He went up the crooked street. He stood at the gate of his yard.

There was a light. It was a lamp light. A lighted lamp was standing in the window of his room.

Paco crossed the yard. Two dark figures were sitting by the kitchen door.

Tío Tomás spoke first. "You have been a long time gone, Señor," he called in his friendly teasing way.

Tía Pita stood up. "Come, my Paco," she said gently. "I've kept your supper waiting. Come in and eat."

79

School began. The Maestro came to see Tomás, to tell Tomás to send young Paco to his school.
The Maestro was tall and thin and very learned. He
knew about books and could tell what they said. The
people of Santa María-of-the-Gardens respected books.
They respected learning. They respected the Maestro.
Paco was in awe of books and learning and the teacher
who taught them. He did not want to go to school.

The Maestro told him, "You must go." Tío Tomás
said, "I want you to go." The Alcalde said, "It is the
law that you go to school." But in the end it was Tía
Pita who made young Paco want to go. She said to the
boy, "The world's magic is in the books. You have only
to get to know them, to make the magic yours."

So Paco went to school, but at first he did not like it.
He felt shy with the other children. He was not used
to children. For as long as he could remember, his
world had been a grown-up world. He liked watching
children from a distance, but he did not know how to
join them in their work or play.

80

Nor was he used to books. Books and reading were unknown to him. He felt ashamed that younger children knew so much more than he knew. School made him feel too unknowing and out-of-place.

It was the Padre who helped him. The Padre had a long talk with the Maestro. He said, "Paco does not belong in your morning school. He knows too much and too little to be with your beginning group. Put him in your afternoon school. He will fit in there. Besides, I need him for that hour each morning to teach him the ways of God."

The Maestro looked pleased. "He is just what I need in my afternoon school," he said. "Justin, *pobrecito*, is too slow at learning. And that José, the other one in afternoon school, is much too fast. Paco, here, knows nothing, but he learns quickly. He is what I need to work with Justin and José."

Paco liked afternoon school. Justin and José were as old and as big as he was. Knowing only as much as Justin and learning as quickly as José made him feel that he belonged. He was an important part of afternoon school.

Lessons were mostly in Spanish because Spanish was the natural language, quick and easy to say and to understand. But lessons were in English also, when the Maestro remembered to give them in English. The Alcalde said that English should be taught, and he

81

showed them in the book he owned where it said that this was the law.

Spanish was easy for Paco. He knew it in his heart. English was more difficult, but he liked learning it. He liked learning to read. He remembered what Pita had told him, that the magic of the world was held in the pages of books and that it could be his when he could read it.

Paco liked school, but he loved his hour with the Padre every morning. The Padre read books to him. Sometimes he read them in English and sometimes in Spanish, but when he talked with the boy, he spoke French. Paco felt more at ease in French. It was his language, the language of his people. It was what the Old One had taught him to speak.

The Padre told the boy many things. He told him the history, the traditions and the customs of the people of Santa María-of-the-Gardens. "These are your people now, Paco, since you have come to live with them. Their beliefs and their ways must be your ways."

Paco nodded. He was content to have it so. His hungry mind could not get enough of knowing what the people did and why they did it.

Autumn work was almost over. The corn had been brought in from the fields. The chili had been picked and strung and hung on the house walls to dry. Halved apricots and squash pieces were drying on the flat roofs. Jerky had been cut in strips and hung over the fence wires. The pinto beans were shelled.

Winter was not far away. The talk now, where people gathered in the fields and the patios and the plaza by the church, was of the Posada, the Christmas custom.

"What is Posada, Father?" Paco asked the Padre. "They talk about it and I do not know what they talk about."

The Padre was glad to tell him. He, too, was thinking of the Posada and wondering who would be the family blessed this year.

"La Posada," he said, "is our Christmas custom, our loveliest custom. It is the acting out of the time before the birth of the Christ Child when Mary and Joseph were trying to find a place of shelter."

The old priest was silent for many minutes, thinking backward to all the Christmases that were now only memory. He had been born in Santa María-of-the-Gardens and had lived there all his life except for his years of study. Those years had been spent in Mexico and France, but they were like dreams now, something that had happened outside his everyday world.

At last he remembered the boy beside him, and continued his story. "We have given this Christmas play for a thousand years. Our people gave it in Spain. When they went to Mexico they took the tradition

83

with them. They gave the Christmas play in Mexico. They brought it with them up the Royal Road from Mexico to Santa Fe, up the Rio Grande to what today is northern New Mexico. At Christmas time from Mexico to Taos, in every mountain Spanish settlement, in every little valley plaza the people give the Christmas play. Each town gives it as they remember it. In each village it may differ a little in the way it is given, but it is the same play, the Christmas play."

The old priest looked at Paco. "There is so much to tell you," he said worriedly. "Our children grow up knowing all these things, but you must learn them. I must teach them to you. This morning I will read to you from the Book. I will read it to you as it has been written."

The Padre got his Book and wiped it carefully and held it in reverence. These words that he was about to read were holy words, not to be read quickly nor without thought.

Paco waited patiently. Long ago he had learned how to wait.

Finally the priest began to read, "And it came to pass in those days that there went out a decree from Caesar Augustus that all the world should be taxed."

Paco listened. "The words are so beautiful," he thought. "They sound almost like a song bird singing."

"And all went to be taxed," the priest read, "everyone into his own city . . . and Joseph also went up from Galilee to be taxed with Mary, his wife. . ."

The Padre looked up from his Book. He looked at the boy who listened so eagerly. ". . . and the Child that was to be born," he said. He was not reading now. He was talking, speaking in French, explaining to the boy the custom of La Posada.

"This was the *Santo Niño,* Paco. He was to be born. But where? There was no room made ready for Him. There was no room at the inn. There was no room in the houses of the town. For eight nights Joseph and Mary and the pilgrims who were with them knocked on doors that would not open. They begged for a place for the Child to be born and received no answer. The doors were closed. The windows were dark. They received no welcome. They were turned away."

Paco sat on the edge of his stool. He could see the houses, dark and unfriendly. He could see the patient Joseph and the frightened Mary.

"Would no one let them in?" he asked. The Padre nodded. "Yes," he answered, "on the ninth night, on Christmas Eve they found a place and the Child was born."

The old priest repeated his words. "They found a place and the Child was born. This is our play, Paco, the Posada of Christmas Eve. We in this village act it out in one night, the twenty-fourth of December. Joseph and Mary are chosen from among our people, and so are the pilgrims. Then lots are cast for the eight houses with the closed doors and for the one house that is blessed to welcome the holy ones."

"Wouldn't it be wonderful to live in the welcoming house?" Paco said softly. The Padre nodded. "It is a wonderful thing to have happen," he said. "Once it happened in my parents' home, once a long time ago when I was very young."

"When do they choose it?" Paco asked. "They do not choose," the priest explained sternly. "Lots are cast. It is the will of God." Then he smiled. "Sunday," he answered. "We have the meeting Sunday after morning Mass."

Paco could not wait to get home to tell Tío Tomás and Tía Pita. "Could it happen to our house?" he asked them excitedly. "It could happen," Tío Tomás answered. "This year or next year or some year," Tía Pita added. "It happens at least once to everyone."

The week dragged by, a week of golden autumn days full of the autumn smells of drying corn and squash and chili.

At last Sunday morning came and Sunday Mass, and after it the meeting. It was held in the schoolhouse with the men sitting on one side of the room and the women and children on the other side. The people were solemn and serious. The children did not talk or play. Even the babies did not cry.

Joseph and Mary were chosen and then the pilgrims who would go with them. The Alcalde tore a paper into small pieces, one for each house in the town of Santa María-of-the-Gardens. On eight pieces the Maestro wrote a number 1 to 8 and on the ninth piece he drew a star. All the papers were folded, the blank ones and ones that had marking on them. The Padre put the pieces in his basket and turned them and tossed them. He put the basket on the table.

Then the men or the boys who had been chosen by their families to represent their houses, formed in a line around the table. Tomás nodded for Paco to join them, and Pita pushed him gently. Suddenly Paco was afraid. He who had never been afraid before was afraid to stand by the basket, to reach out and pick the piece of paper that could mean so much to him.

In the end, Tomás went with him. "I will stand behind you, Paco, to give you courage. But you are the one to pick up the paper."

The schoolroom was quiet, quiet. Not a breath stirred. Brown hands reached into the basket. Bits of white paper fluttered in steady brown fingers. All but Paco's fingers. They trembled. They were not steady. Blindly he turned to Pita. "Read it, Tía, read it," he

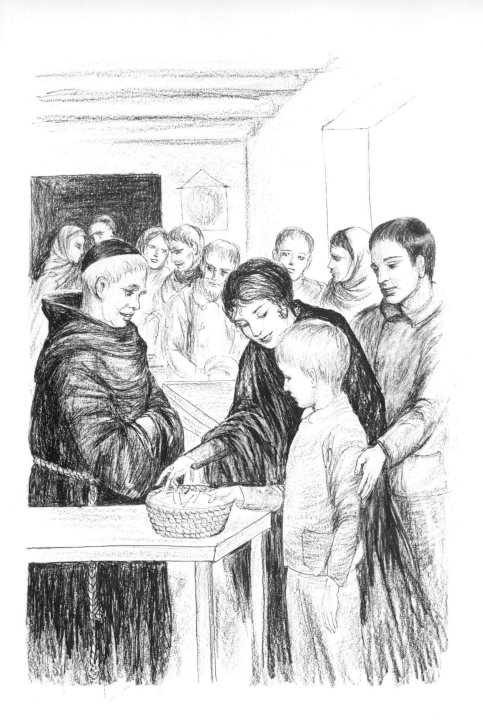

whispered. "No," Tía Pita told him. "You must read it. You represent our family."

Paco opened the paper. "It has the star," he whispered. "It is the will of God," the people said.

There was rejoicing and thanksgiving in the house of Tío Tomás. All through the hours of afternoon and evening there was rejoicing and thanksgiving. There was, also, talk and worry.

"There must be wood for the Christmas fires and candles for the window light," Tío Tomás said.

"There must be paper flowers for the *Santo Niño* and food for the guests," Tía Pita said.

"We have so little money." Tomás sounded very sad.

"We have food," Paco said loudly. "We have corn and chili and squash and beans and jerky." He could not bear to have Tío Tomás speak sadly. But it did not help.

"Candles and paper flowers, cookies and chocolate cost money. Our house must have warmth and light. It must be beautiful and welcoming for the *Santo Niño*," Tomás told him, shaking his head with worry.

"But you forget," Tía Pita said, "this has been the will of God. He will help us. We have no worries and it is time for bed."

Paco was not so sure. He went to bed, but it was a long time before he slept.

91

As happened, always, every morning Paco wakened to the sound of Pita's singing. He would hear the slap, slap as she flapped and patted the breakfast tortillas.

As happened, always, every morning happiness flooded the boy's heart, happiness that this place was his home and this family was his family.

At first this morning he thought only of Tía Pita's singing and the slap, slap of her tortilla-making and the beating of his happy heart.

Then he remembered. He remembered the meeting last night. He remembered how he had picked the paper with the star. Excitement ran through him like a forest fire as he thought of what had happened. This house, his house, the house that he had helped to build would be this year's shelter for the Christ Child's coming.

He remembered, also, the talking afterward. He remembered Tío Tomás' worry because they had no money for the things they would need to buy.

Last night, Paco had joined his uncle in his worry. But this morning, listening to Tía Pita's singing, he could not bring it back again. That this house had been the chosen one, was the will of God. It had to be. How else could he have picked the paper with the star? It was the will of God and Tía Pita had said that God would send them the help they needed. He would make something happen. Paco felt sure of it.

So he dressed. As he dressed he whistled in tune with Tía Pita's singing.

When he went into the kitchen, a surprise was there Tía Carmen, Tomás' sister, and her husband, Tío Carlos, had come to visit. Such an early morning visit was a thing of great importance. Paco wondered what it was.

Carlos and Tomás sat in silence. Tío Tomás still was worried. Paco could see the worry on his uncle's face. Tío Carlos sat in silence because he did not know what else to do. He did not know why he was there, at Tomás' house. He did not know why they had come, so early in the morning.

Tía Pita had stopped her singing. She and Tía Carmen were chatting like magpies. They talked gaily of this and that and that and this, but not, Paco knew of what they were thinking.

Pita kneaded more tortilla dough. Since they would have company for breakfast, they would need more

93

tortillas. She patted and slapped the dough into plate-size round tortillas. She baked them on the hot tin in the fireplace. She stacked them on the breakfast plates. She poured strong black coffee into the coffee cups.

Tomás asked the blessing. The family and their visitors sat down to eat.

Carmen said, "Pita, there is a way." Pita looked down at her plate. She tore pieces of her tortilla and folded them neatly into bite-size bits. "Yes," she said. "I've thought of it, too. It's the only thing to do."

For a second Paco thought she was crying. But in a little time, she looked up again. Paco looked at her closely. She had the usual twinkle in her shining eyes. She had the usual smile of mischief on her pretty face. Paco sighed with relief. The world was right again. His Tía Pita had not been crying.

Pita was looking at Tomás. She was smiling at him. "Where did you get the money to buy the lumber and the nails and the rafters for our beautiful house?" she asked him.

Tomás was surprised. Pita knew where and how he had got the money. But if Pita asked him, it was right that he should answer her. So he said, as duty told him to say, "You know, my María Pita, you know that I worked in Santa Fe for wages. You know that is where I got the money." He added proudly, "Santa Fe is a good place to work for money. No, Carlos? Remember, you went there, too."

94

Carlos laughed. "Of course," he said, "of course I remember. We were *ricos* when we worked in Santa Fe." Carmen smiled at him. "That's where my Carlito got the money to buy my cow and chickens," she boasted.

Now that Carlos had started talking, he could not stop. "Santa Fe is the place to make money. You need some, go get it. All you have to do is work two, three months and you have money in your pocket."

"The Alcalde told me," Carmen said, "that men are needed for road work in Santa Fe this winter. The mail stage brought some men from Taos who were going there."

Pita looked at Carmen. Her eyes were black pools in her still face. But now that she had started the talking, she too could not stop it. "*Santo Niño,*" she whispered in her heart. "I do this for Your welcome." Aloud she said, looking at Carmen, "Two months and only a few days and it will be time for the Christmas Posada."

Carmen looked surprised. "Two months," she repeated. "Four paydays. Think of the money four paydays could bring. Think of the things the money would buy."

Tomás flushed. He looked at Pita. "It's the only thing to do," he told her.

Pita could not answer, but Carmen helped him. "Did you know," she spoke to Pita, "that my Carlito is going to Santa Fe to work with your Tomás? It will not be so bad for you if there are two of us here to miss them."

It was Carlos' turn to be surprised. "I am?" he asked. "I am going where? Where is Tomás going?"

"To Santa Fe," Carmen laughed. "To work for wages. To buy things for La Posada."

Before they knew it, both men were planning what they would buy with money earned from two months' work. "Candles, store candles, and colored paper for flowers and a gift for the *Santo Niño*," Tomás promised. "Cookies that come in boxes and sweet water that comes in bottles," Carlos told Carmen. "I, myself, will buy those things and we will give them for the *Santo Niño*, will we not, my Carmencita?"

Tomás looked worried. "I cannot leave you, Pita. Who would bring you wood and water?"

"I would," Paco promised. "Paco will do it," Carmen said. "Paco will take care of Pita while you are gone."

"It takes much wood in winter time." Tomás still was worried. "Sometimes you need to go high up on the mountain slope."

"I know the mountains," Paco answered proudly.

It was Carlos' turn to worry. "No, no, no, no. What am I thinking of?" he shouted. "I cannot go. Who is there to milk our cow and take the Padre and his cat their pitcher of milk each morning?"

"I could," Paco promised. "Paco can do it," Carmen said. "He is a big boy and gentle with animals."

"She will try to horn you, Paco, and kick you," Carlos worried. "She has tried it on me. She will try it with you."

"I know animals—perhaps not cows, but other animals," Paco said quietly. "I am not afraid."

At last it was decided. The men would go. They would go in the mail stage when it came by next week. They would come back in it a week before Christmastime.

Tomás was sad. He did not want to go, but he hid his sadness from Pita. It was right that he should go where there was money to be earned. It was right that they should have beautiful things for La Posada. Pita must never know what leaving her would cost him.

Pita cried every night. But she dried her tears at the first light of morning. The *Santo Niño* must have a proper welcome. There was no other way to get it for Him. Tomás must never knew how much she would miss him.

Paco had many feelings. He was happy that his house was the house with the star. He was proud that his Tío Tomás could work for wages in Santa Fe. He felt important that he was the one to take care of Tía Pita, and of Tía Carmen's cow.

Pita washed and ironed Tomás' clothes and packed them in a bright blue suitcase made of tin. She cooked corn and chili, beans and squash for him to take, and

put them in a clean, white flour sack. She sang only when Tomás asked her to sing. She laughed only when Tomás teased her to laughter.

Mail day and the mail stage came too soon, it seemed to Tomás and to Pita. They said good-by inside their house and walked without words to the plaza where the stage was waiting.

Now that it was time to go, Carlos did not want to go. He stayed as long as he could, talking to Carmen. Tomás climbed inside at once, and at last Carlos followed him. The driver flicked his whip. The stage wheels creaked in turning.

Carmen cried, but Pita did not cry. She stood proud and silent. Silently she watched the stage rumble across the plaza, through the river and along the road to Santa Fe.

Silently she walked home with Paco. Paco had not known that he would miss Tío Tomás. He had not known how heavy his heart would be.

Supper was a lonely meal. The evening was long and quiet.

IN the morning, Paco was the first to waken. Now that he was the man of Tomás' house, he must do the work of Tomás.

He went to the well in the plaza to get Pita her day's supply of water. He chopped the wood for the fireplace fires. After breakfast he went to Carmen's house to water and feed and milk the cow. He brought the milk into the house to Carmen. Then he took some for Pita and some for the Padre and the Padre's cat.

He went to the mountain slope for wood and dragged it down through the snow. Always, every day, he saw the wild dog. No matter which way he went, the wild one was there waiting for him. It watched him, watched him, but when he called it would not come.

These days there was more than a hint of winter. The mountains were white with snow, and frost lay heavy in the valley.

From the first, Paco had trouble with Carmen's cow. Pita warned him, "Be careful. That silly cow may horn you." Carmen warned him, "Be careful. That silly cow will be sure to kick you. She always kicked poor Carlos."

But this was not the trouble. The cow did not horn him. She did not kick him. She followed him home. No matter how tight he wired the gate at Carmen's house, the cow pushed it or opened it or jumped it, and followed him home. When he came from the Padre's house, the cow would be waiting for him. He would speak crossly to it and take it back to Carmen's house. When he came from school, when he came back from wood gathering, the cow would be waiting for him. Even on Sunday when he came from Mass, there the cow stood at the church door chewing her cud and waiting for him.

Finally Pita said, "Put that silly cow in the lean-to Tomás built." Carmen said, "Yes. Take that silly cow over to your house. That's what she wants. She will be happy there."

Surprisingly, this proved true. The cow seemed happy in the lean-to. She waited there contentedly for Paco to come to her.

Secretly, Paco was pleased. He had wanted an animal in the lean-to. That was why Tomás had built it. "Some day," he had said, "perhaps we will have an animal here." The boy brought hay from Carmen's house. The cow must have plenty to eat.

101

Snow fell every night, but it was only flurries, soft and clean in morning and melted in midday.

The mail stage came again, bringing letters from Tomás—a long one for Pita, a shorter one for Paco. It was Paco's first letter. He could read it, at first with a little help but later by himself. Old Pierre was well, Tomás wrote. He liked Santa Fe. He liked the Sisters. He wanted to stay there the rest of his days. Paco could come to see him in the summer. Tomás had written that he himself would take Paco to Santa Fe to see the Old One. He wrote, "The Old One, as you know, talks much, but not too clearly. But this he says over and over: 'The young Paco has a heritage. Tell him I say be true to his name until the end of his days.' I do not know," Tomás had written, "what he means by this, but you must know, and this I have told him."

Paco thought he knew what the Old One meant. He spoke softly to the birds, feeding them corn. They did not seem to hear him.

Then he read his letter again. The Old One was happy. That was a comfort. Tío Tomás would be home in three weeks. It would be wonderful having Tío Tomás home again.

Pita, too, was pleased with her letter from Tomás. Looking forward to three weeks was a long time, but looking back, once it was over, would be very short. Pita knew this. She sang again.

Everyone in Santa María-of-the-Gardens was busy getting ready for Christmas. The eight houses where the *Santo Niño* was not welcome were cleaned and freshened. Even though, this year, these houses were not blessed to receive the Child, they were still important. They had a part in the age-old La Posada Christmas play.

Mary and Joseph rehearsed their parts. The pilgrims practiced their holy songs. Paco and Tía Pita carried on, waiting for the day Tío Tomás would return with the wonderful things he would bring for the Christ Child's welcome.

Another mail day came with another letter from Tío Tomás. Only ten days more, he wrote, until he would be with them. Ten more breakfasts, ten more suppers, ten more lonely evenings and he would be back again.

Then it began to snow. Big beautiful snowflakes swirled and turned and fell lazily, slowly, steadily downward. The streets and the fields were white. Snow banked in the house yards and drifted across the plaza.

School was closed. Children stayed indoors. Only Paco went to the well for water, went to the Padre's house with the pitcher of milk, went to the mountain slopes for wood.

Tonight, he was very late getting the wood supply. It had taken a long time to plough through the waist-deep snowdrifts. It had taken a long time to find the wood he needed. It had taken even longer to dig it from the frozen snowbank and drag it down the drifted snow slopes. He walked slowly, dragging the wood behind him. His head was bent. His eyes were on the snowdrifts to safeguard against falling. He bumped into the grey object in the greyer dusk before he saw it or knew it was there. It moved slightly against the weight of his body. Paco jumped backward, his heart in his throat. After a breathless moment he dared look more closely. The animal was a burro, lost, lonely, cold, standing patiently in the falling snow.

Paco brushed the snow from the furry sides. He patted it gently. He talked to it softly. Paco did not know burros very well, although the Alcalde's oldest son owned three of them. But they were dark brown and this one was grey. Even in the failing light, Paco could see its grey furry coat.

He tried to lead the burro. The burro would not lead. He tried to push it. It would not budge. It was getting late and very dark. Snow was still falling. Finally in despair the boy gave up. He went on, dragging his wood, his thin body bending against the falling snow. He had not gone far when he realized that the burro followed him.

The boy did not dare look back. He did not dare to stop. He went slowly on, step by step through the night and the snow.

104

At last he came to his gate. He went through it. The burro followed him. He went into the lean-to. The burro followed him.

Tía Pita came to the door to call softly, "Paco, you are very late. Is everything all right with you?" Paco laughed. He did not feel tired nor cold, now that he was home and the burro was in the lean-to. "Look what I brought home with me, Tía Pita. Bring the lantern and look what I have here."

When Pita came she cried in pleased surprise, "A burro, Paco, for Mary to ride for La Posada." But with a second breath, she asked, "Where is the man who owns it?" "The man?" Paco did not understand. He had not thought that the man who owned the burro might be back there, somewhere, on the mountain slope. He had thought only of the burro. There must be a man. Burros do not come alone. Someone comes with them.

Tiredly he turned away and began the long walk back up the mountain slope. He heard someone behind him. It was Pita hurrying through the snow, trying to catch up with him. "You must not come, Tía. There is too much snow. It is too far, too cold." "I am coming," Pita answered. "Tío Tomás would not like for you to come, my Tía," Paco said gently. "Tomás would expect me to come," Pita said and then, more gently, "I am a woman, now, my Paco. I go where my family needs me."

Paco could not answer. Words caught in his throat. Silently he turned and began to climb the trail. Wrapped in her Sunday shawl, carrying the lantern, Pita trudged behind him as he ploughed through the drifted snow.

It was more than an hour before they found what they were looking for. The traveler was an old man with a brown, wrinkled face and a beard as white as the snow around him. He had slipped and fallen and hurt his ankle. Now he lay across his pack, half frozen, not caring what would happen.

"He's a trader," Pita whispered. "Perhaps from Mexico. Lost in the storm." She bent over the old man. "You are with friends, Señor," she said in Spanish. "Your burrito is safe. We will take you to it."

For a long time the boy and the woman worked with the old man. They rubbed his face, his hands, his feet with snow. They made him stand. After a while he seemed to know what they were doing. He seemed to want to help them get him to their home. But he could not walk alone. He had to be helped. Pita walked beside him down the narrow, slippery, snow-filled trail. Paco dragged the heavy pack and lighted the trail with the lantern. The going was slow and painful.

107

Day was breaking through the snowclouds when they reached home again.

The burro in the lean-to brayed loudly. The cow moved restlessly, and in the shadows the wild dog watched the boy he loved.

Paco ached with tiredness. He was stiff with cold, but he felt very proud. He was proud of himself, that he could do what needed to be done. He was proud of Pita that she was brave and strong when courage and strength were needed. He was proud that the lean-to he had helped to build was dry and warm for the animals it sheltered.

Pita bandaged the old man's ankle. She coaxed him to drink strong, black coffee. She fixed a blanket bed close to the kitchen fireplace.

Looking down at the old man, Paco felt tenderness fill his heart. Suddenly he knew a great truth. He knew that pride can come from a feeling of strength but that tenderness is a sign of manhood.

Pita, glancing up, said in a tone of wonderment, "Paco, you are growing up. You are not just a little boy like you were a month ago."

Paco smiled at her. He went out to get more wood for the fireplace. The old trader would need a warm place to sleep.

It was only nine days until Christmas Eve and the coming of the *Santo Niño*.

109

AT first, the Trader would not talk to Paco or to Pita. He sat hunched by the fireplace all day, and unrolled his blanket close to the fire at night. He seemed old and tired and cold. Even his heart seemed cold, locked in frozen stillness. He was indifferent to Paco's friendliness, to Pita's gentle care and to the food she prepared for him and coaxed him to eat. Only two things were of interest to him, the warmth of the fire and the welfare of his burro. He needed to know, constantly, how his burro was faring.

Perhaps it was the Trader's concern for his burro that brought about his recovery, for the burro and Paco became friends. They became companions.

When Paco was in the house, the burro looked in the window. At first this startled Pita, but finally she became used to seeing the long-eared burro looking through the window glass.

When Paco went outside, the burro followed him around. Now that the cow knew that she was living in Paco's lean-to, she was content to stand and watch him. But not the burro. The burro wanted to be where

110

Paco was. It wanted to go where Paco went. If it could not find Paco, it brayed in loneliness until the boy returned.

This pleased the Trader. He seemed to understand and accept his burro's devotion to the boy. That Paco returned the burrito's affection added to his pleasure.

Gradually the old man got better. He became more friendly. He ate what Pita prepared for him and was grateful for her care. His ankle became less painful and less swollen. He hobbled about with the aid of his pilgrim's staff. Being able to get around made him willing to leave the fire. He moved his blanket to the lean-to and seemed happy to be out there, sleeping beside his burro in the warm, dry shelter.

During the day, the Trader did little chores for *la Señora*. In the evenings he would come into the house for a while, sit by the fire and tell stories. The evenings became less lonely with the Trader's tales of his trading adventures.

He came once a year, he told them, up the Royal Road from Mexico to Taos. He brought buttons and pins and calico, cinnamon and chocolate and water flavors to trade in Taos for animal pelts. Before this time, he had never come to Santa María-of-the-Gardens. It was somewhat off the trail. Besides, he had not needed to come. All that he and his burro could pack, he could trade in Taos with the people there.

111

This year, winter had come early. Shortly after leaving Taos, snow had fallen and he was unprepared for it. Also, the Trader said, his burrito had strayed in the night, something it had never done before. Tracking it, the Trader had become lost in the snow-filled valleys.

"I think he knew that you were here, Paco, and would find us and bring us to shelter and food," the Trader said. He believed it. He believed that his burro had planned to come here to the house where Paco lived.

Paco laughed. He was embarrassed, but he was pleased. "Now that he helps me carry hay from Tía Carmen's house and water and wood, I can bring all that is needed. I can bring water and wood to Tía Carmen, too. It is your burro who helps us, Señor."

The days passed slowly. There was no let-up in the falling snow. Day and night it fell softly, thickly, steadily. The sky, the land, the whole world seemed blanketed in snowclouds and snowdrifts. There was no wind. There was no sound. There was only snow, snow, snow. Only the different shapes of the things it covered gave reality to an empty, snow-filled world.

Tuesday, Wednesday, Thursday, Paco and the burro ploughed through the drifts to get wood and water. They ploughed through the drifts to Tía Carmen's house to bring her the pails of milk and to take back hay for the cow and the burro. They ploughed through the drifts to take the pitcherfuls of milk to the Padre and his cat. Twice the cat tried to follow them. Scolding her gently, Paco carried her back through the snow and put her in the house where she belonged. Then he trudged back again to where the patient burro waited for him and together they went home.

Pita began to worry. Five days were left until the day of La Posada. That was all. Five days until Christmas Eve.

Friday, the Padre came. He was carrying his cat. "She followed me," he told Pita. "I was almost here before I knew it." He put the cat on the floor. "Go to the fire," he told her. "Get your feet dry. You know how you dislike getting them wet. I don't know why you came."

The cat went immediately to Paco, rubbing against his feet and purring loudly. The old Padre laughed. "She likes you, Paco. I think that's why she came."

The Padre laughed again, but, turning to Pita, the laughter left him. He looked worried. "I have had no news about road conditions from either Santa Fe or Taos. An Indian runner was supposed to come by yesterday. He did not come. I cannot understand it. An Indian runner can always get through." The Padre picked up his cat and petted her. He shook his head.

"I can't understand it. I can't understand it," he said.

He looked at Pita. Pita was sewing. She did not look up. The Padre kept on talking. "Of course there is no mail. No stage could get through these drifts, but the runner should have been able to get through."

Pita asked the Padre in her quiet voice if he would have a cup of coffee. She did not tell him that there was little coffee left. She did not tell him that fear held her heart so tightly that pain was with her constantly. "A cup of coffee, Father, will be good for you," she coaxed him.

"No, no. No coffee, thank you. I just happened to be passing by and came in for a minute." Then, knowing how unbelievable that must sound since he had fought snowbank and snowdrift to get here, he changed his words. "Well, anyway, I came and now I must go back. God be with you, María Pita. He will send us word tomorrow."

Pita went to the door with him and watched him, a blurred shape, quickly become lost in the falling snow. Then she came back to the fire again to sew and to think her silent thoughts.

Saturday, Sunday, the snow did not stop. Everyone, Sunday morning, went to Mass as usual. Snowdrifts nor snowbanks nor snow clouds could not keep them home. They came through the streets in family groups. The fathers came first, making the tracks for the children to follow. The mothers were last, to pick up the little ones who fell, to comfort them and urge them on. They came through the streets and across the plaza. They came into the church, breathless and cold. They knelt before the altar where the Santa María looked down at them. She would help them. Through the centuries she had guarded and protected them. She would help them now.

They bowed their heads in prayer. The Padre said the Mass. The snow kept falling.

MONDAY there was some relief. The snow
did not stop, not entirely. But there were moments
throughout the day when the sun shone through the
grey snow clouds. It shone not too brightly, not too
long, but each time staying longer, giving stronger
hope.

The day began with visitors. Carmen came first. She
brought a basket of eggs. "From my hens to Paco," she
said teasing him, "to thank him for the corn he has
been bringing to them." She smiled at Pita.

They knew, both of them, that the eggs were to be
used for La Posada fiesta. They knew that if their men
did not get back in time, the party food would be
scarce and poor. They knew that their cupboards as
well as those of their neighbors were almost empty.
But they did not say what they knew. They did not
say what they feared. Such words they would never
say.

So Carmen teased Paco and she teased Pita. "Next
time you send your Tomás away to work, it had better

118

be in summertime," she laughed. She laughed gaily to show that she had no worries, no worries about anything.

Pita smiled back at her husband's sister. She was glad of the friendship that tied their lives together. She was thankful that here was a friend who knew and shared the fear that lay frozen in her heart. They knew this fear and shared it, but would never speak of it. Words might unlock the gate that held it, and, running wild, it might possess them.

Pita gave her sister-in-law a cup of coffee-*con-leche*. She did not offer sugar for its sweetening. There was no sugar. The sugar sack had long been empty. Carmen did not ask for sugar. She did not mention it. There was no sugar at her house, either. There was no coffee. She had nothing left but corn and chili. The eggs she had brought she could have used at home. They were a precious gift. But she did not say this. They did not talk about food.

They did not talk about the snow nor the nearness of La Posada. They knew these things. Why talk about them? Why not talk about happy things?

Carmen teased Paco about his friends, the cow and the burro. "I hear that even the Padre's cat wants to come and live at this house," she said. Paco did not mind Tía Carmen's teasing. He knew that she liked him. This was her way of showing it.

119

Carmen asked questions about the Trader. She wanted to know everything about him that there was to know. "You are lucky to have someone to talk to you," she told Pita and Paco. "My babies are too little to talk to me. I am going to learn how to talk to myself."

So Carmen asked questions and Pita answered them. They were having a wonderful visit when Pita's mother came. She brought one of Pita's sisters with her. Paco was pleased. Pita's sister was his special friend.

"Mama," Pita cried. "Mama, I am so glad to see you. But how did you get here with the snow so deep and the drifts so high?"

"On my two feet," Mama answered. Then, to get to the business of her visit quickly, she asked, "What are you doing about Posada?"

Pita looked at her mother. She could not answer. Words caught in her throat. The fear beat in her heart. Paco spoke loudly. "Tío Tomás will come, *Abuela*. He is bringing everything we need." He added proudly, "He will buy them with his money. He will have much money."

Mama was not to be stopped by such a silly statement. Tomás was not here. Probably it would be impossible for him to get here. It was too bad, but it could not be helped. What was important was La

Posada. This house of her daughter had been the chosen house to receive the Christ Child. It was an honor not to be cast aside. The house must be a proper place to receive Him. It must be warm with cedar fire. It must be bright with candlelight. It must be beautiful with Christmas decorations. There must be fiesta food for the guests. There must be sweet cakes. There must be a sweet drink.

"Have you made your Christmas cookies, María Pita?" Mama asked.

"No, Mama."

"I have this small pail of wheat flour. It will make a few. Not many. A panful, perhaps."

"Thank you, Mama," Pita murmured.

Pita's mother looked at her daughter. Something was wrong. She thought she knew what it was. She would find out if what she thought was true. She asked, "María Pita, how much wheat flour have you?" There was no answer. "Do you have any wheat flour, María Pita?"

"No, Mama," Pita answered.

"Do you have sugar?"

"No, Mama."

Mama threw up her hands. "Well, Papa says you are to get what you need from the store. It is what Tomás would want you to do."

Pita's answer was lost. The Padre was at the door. His cat was gone. "Is she here?" he asked. "Did she come here? Have you seen her?"

No one had seen the Padre's cat. But before they could answer, the Trader came hobbling in. He pointed with his thumb to the dooryard. "They have come," he said. "They must have news."

Everyone rushed to the door. The Padre and his cat were forgotten. Coming through the yard was the Alcalde and the Postmaster.

"Speak up," the Padre called to them. "Do you have news? What news do you bring?"

"Sí, Padre. We have news," the men said coming into the house, stamping the snow from their feet, clapping their hands to get them warm. "The Indian runner has come. He is on his way to Taos. There has been a snowslide at the Pass. He got through only seconds before the slide. It will take many men many hours to dig through."

"Were men caught in the slide?" the Padre asked. The Alcalde shook his head. "The runner said the men had not reached the Pass when the slide came." The Padre asked another question, "When the men reach the Pass, will they be able to dig through?" Again the Alcalde answered, "If the snow stops, they can make it by tomorrow. I will have horses waiting for them on this side."

123

The Postmaster looked at Pita. He spoke to her. "It is but a short way, María Pita. If the snow stops, Tomás and Carlos can get here in time."

The Storekeeper had come, too, but in the excitement no one had seen him. He had been standing close to the door. When the Padre went out, Mama saw him and began talking at once. "Alfonso," she said, "I am glad you have come. This child has neither flour nor sugar to make the Christmas sweet cakes. Her papa says to give them to her. Tomás will pay you."

The Storekeeper wrung his hands. His face showed his misery. "Señora, Señora," he cried, "I do not have them. All my barrels are empty. I, too, was expecting the mail stage to bring supplies. Candles and matches I have and these I have brought in good amount. These I gladly give to María Pita."

Mama was furious. "You do not give her the wheat flour and the sugar that she needs?"

"Señora, Señora, how can I give her what I do not have?" the Storekeeper cried in sorrow. He looked at Mama. He knew she would not believe him. "I haven't even a cupful of anything," he said sadly.

The Trader dragged in his packsack. "I have chocolate and cinnamon," he boasted, "enough for *la Señora* and the fiesta."

Carmen said, "I brought the eggs to thicken the chocolate with beaten egg whites. There is milk here."

124

Mama snorted. "Chocolate and cinnamon, egg whites and milk are not enough. One needs sugar for chocolate. Much sugar. It must be very sweet. And what about the sweet cakes? One needs wheat flour and sugar for sweet cakes."

Pita began to cry. "I have no paper for the paper flowers. I have no gift for the *Santo Niño,* and Tomás will not be here," she wailed.

Mama looked at her daughter. Her heart cried for her, but this was no time to show her tears. Spanish ladies were Spanish ladies when things went well. When things went badly they must remember that they were the women of Spanish conquerors and, if need be, fought beside their men.

Mama shrugged her shoulders. She tossed her head. She said with spirit, "You will remember, Daughter, that your house has been chosen for La Posada. You will receive Mary and Joseph and the Holy Child with grace and dignity."

She motioned for Pita's sister and for Carmen to precede her through the door. She said to the Alcalde and the Postmaster, to the Storekeeper and the Trader, "You are leaving? So nice that you came." Mama smiled graciously, but she waited until she could close the door behind them. Then she, too, left. Paco saw her wipe her eyes as she turned her back on Pita.

Tears streamed down Pita's face. She was not

125

ashamed to cry. Between her sobs, she said, "I am tired, my Paco. I want to go to my room. Can you cook the supper for the Trader and yourself?"

"Yes, Tía. I can cook it," Paco said. He brushed his hand across his eyes. He tried to cook, but the corn tortillas burned and the chili scorched. It did not matter. He was not hungry. The Trader would not eat.

In the lean-to the cow kicked the bucket when the Trader tried to milk her. The burro brayed and brayed.

Inside the house the lamp flickered and smoked The coal oil was low. Paco blew out the light and for a while sat in the dim glow of the smoldering fire. He thought about the mountain top that for so many years, wintertime and summertime, had been his home. All the winters that he could remember had been long and cold and snow filled. But there had never been a winter as bad as this one. Perhaps it had been such a winter as this one that had wiped out the French settlement in the valley beyond. He thought of it as the French settlement. He never thought of the place as home. But thinking backward now brought memories of Pierre, the Old One, and the mountain top where they had lived.

Shadows lengthened in the room. The night grew colder. Paco wiped his eyes and blew his nose. Then, banking the fire for the night, he went to bed.

126

The night outside was black. The house was dark. There was no light shining through the window of Tía Pita's room.

After a long time, Paco went to sleep.

Then the dream came. It was a strange dream, not clear, not understandable, but one that directed, demanded and compelled.

Paco turned in his sleep. He was restless. Sleep was not quiet nor peaceful. He turned and twisted. The dream came back again. It was more commanding this time, more compelling.

At last the boy, still sleeping, staggered from his bed to obey the dream.

Snow had stopped falling. A pale moon looked down in sorrow upon the frozen world.

The night passed slowly, slowly. In some far canyon coyotes barked. The wild dog moaned.

Pita sat up in bed. She was still sobbing, although sleep had eased somewhat the heaviness in her heart.

The room was grey and shadowy. Something had wakened her. She listened, listened. Then she heard the sound again. What was it? Where did it come from? She listened, listened. She heard it again. It was a scratching at the door.

Quickly she ran to the door and opened it. Her sobs had stopped. She was not crying now. She felt calm

127

and strong. This was danger of some kind. She knew it. She felt ready to meet it.

Looking out into the grey mist of morning, she saw nothing. She looked down at the floor of the portal. Then she saw it. She saw the wild dog. It was the wild dog. Instantly she knew it was the wild dog that Paco loved.

The dog looked up at her. She knew that it was not afraid of her, but it was afraid of something. There was fear in its eyes. There was fear and pleading. It was begging her for help.

Pita ran to Paco's room. It was as she had thought. The room was empty. Paco had gone. There was no one there. There was no one in his bed. His blanket was gone.

Quickly she wrapped her shawl around her, lighted the lantern with trembling fingers. The wild dog was waiting when she came out again. It went before her, looking back constantly to see if she followed. They went through the gate, down the street and to the foot of the mountain where the trail began. It was then that Pita realized that the little burro walked behind her.

Paco's friends and Paco's Tía stumbled through the snow. They did not have far to go. Almost at once they found him. They found the young boy lying face down in the snow.

128

He had gone where the dream had demanded that he go. He had done what the dream had directed that he do. Then he had started down the homeward trail, but exhaustion and cold had caught up with him. He had fallen in the snow. He lay sleeping, where he had fallen.

Pita had a difficult time in wakening him, in beating back life into his almost frozen body. At last she got him on his feet. She pushed him toward the burro. She lifted him upon the burro's back. She had a harder time in getting his blanket bundle up behind him and in tying it to him and around the burro.

"Why did you go?" she asked over and over. "Why did you go?" He answered, "I don't know. . . . A dream, I think." She asked him, "What is in your blanket? What do you have in your blanket?" His only answer was, "I don't know. . . . For you, I think."

With the wild dog to guide her and the burro to carry him, it did not take long to get Paco home, to untie him from the burro and to put him to bed.

The wild dog came into the house as if it had belonged there always. It was not afraid, but neither was it friendly. It came with quiet dignity and Pita accepted it with quiet dignity. They understood each other. They needed each other.

After Paco was safe in bed, Pita went out for the blanket bundle. She dragged it into the house. She untied it. She looked at the things it held. She touched them. They were the treasures that Paco had gone to the mountain to get. He had got them for her because she wanted them, she needed them.

These things were his gift to her. But he had given her an even greater gift. He had taught her how and what to value.

"Tomás, Tomás," she cried brokenly. "That I should have sent you to earn money to buy things when all we needed to have to honor Him, He had given us already in our valley and on our mountain."

CHAPTER THIRTEEN

WHEN Paco opened his eyes again, it was midday. He was in his own room with a bright fire crackling and dancing in the fireplace. The noisy fire and the smell of burning cedar wood were friendly things to waken him, he thought. Then he sniffed again. He wrinkled his nose with deep smelling. Mingling with the smell of cedar was the smell of sweet cakes baking on the earthernware pan in the kitchen fireplace.

Instantly, the boy was reminded of the happenings of the night before. Which of these were real, and which were dreams, he wondered. He tried to remember clearly. He tried to sort the happenings into neat little packages of those things which happened when he was awake and those other things which were just a dream. But he could not do it. He could not be sure that anything at all had happened. Perhaps everything had been a dream.

Suddenly he realized that someone, something was with him in his room. Slowly he turned his head and

looked into the yellow-brown eyes of the wild dog.
Even in his great astonishment, the boy knew that he
must move slowly, speak gently, must in no way
frighten or confuse the wild one that at last had come
to him.

The door opened softly. Tía Pita came in. The wild
dog looked at her, but briefly, then turned to look
deeply into the eyes of his accepted master.

"Everything is all right, Paco," Tía Pita said. "Your
dog has come to share your home. He even ate when
I fed him this morning."

"When did he come, Tía Pita?" Paco was almost
afraid to ask.

"With us, when I brought you back this morning,"
Tía Pita answered.

So, Paco thought. At least the edges of the dream
had been real. Some of it had happened. Aloud he
said, slowly, softly touching the wild one's head, "Good
dog. Good dog." Then, looking at Pita, he said, "Tía,
tell me about last night. Not all of it was dreaming,
was it?"

"Not now, Paco," Pita answered. "Tomorrow will be
time for talking. But the rest of today is for the *Santo
Niño*. Come see what you have done for the Holy In-
fant and for me."

Pita turned toward the door, then stopped. "Paco."
She hesitated. Then she began again. "Paco, the wild

one came to you. He has not come lightly. He has come to stay. But do not forget, my Pacocito, that in small ways he will always be wild. Do not try to tame him completely or to keep him entirely. Let him always be a little wild and very free."

Tía Pita went out and closed the door behind her.

Paco knew what she meant. He had known in his heart that he must do this. It was a comfort to know that Tía Pita also knew. He could be sure of her help if he needed it.

He went to the door, opened it and stood there, waiting. The wild dog leaped forward, then came back for a heartbeat second to press his head against the boy's hand. By the time Paco had wiped his hand across his eyes, and could see again, the dog was gone.

Snow had stopped falling. The sky was as blue as on a summer day. The afternoon sun shone brightly warm. Only the snowdrifts and snowbanks and snow-covered trees gave proof that for more than a week, storms had raged upon the mountain top and in the canyons and the valley.

Paco wondered where Tío Tomás was, if they had cut through the Pass and if they would be home tomorrow.

The Trader spoke. Paco had not known that anyone was near. "By San Martine, I swear it. You've got yourself a dog," the old man said. Paco looked where his dog had gone, but saw nothing but his tracks in the snow. "Will he be back?" Paco asked the Trader.

"Will he be back?" the Trader laughed. "He will be back. Always, always he will go, but always, also, he will come back again."

Paco remembered his own trip back to the mountain top a month ago. He heard again Tía Pita's words as she told him, "The mountain trail is not a trail that you walk but once. It is a pathway between two homes." This was true with him. It would be true for Wild Dog. The words brought deep and lasting comfort.

The boy went into the kitchen and stopped in amazement. The room had been turned into a fairyland of beauty. The walls were hung with branches of juniper, heavy with berries, and grey-green lacey-tipped cedar. Bunches of mistletoe with tiny pearl-pink berries hung from the rafters. Bunches of kinni-kinnick were everywhere; the waxy green leaves and bright red berries gave the room a festive Christmas look.

The kitchen table had been turned into a shrine to receive the *Santo Niño*. It was covered with the embroidered shawl from Spain that had been in Pita's wedding chest. Her ivory fan, her gold comb, her filigree necklace made fitting decoration.

136

Paco could not say a word nor could he not stop looking. Another bit of his dream had given way to this that was real.

Mama had come back and so had Carmen. Both of them were in the kitchen. Both of them were working. Carmen was shelling piñons, roasting them and sticking them into the sweet tortilla cakes that Mama was making.

"I see you are using piñons," Paco said to Tía Carmen. To his grandmother he asked, "Are you using wheat flour, *Abuela?*"

Mama laughed. "There is no wheat flour in all the town of Santa María-of-the-Gardens. We are using an old-time recipe that calls for cornmeal, honey and piñons."

"Honey?" Paco asked. "Honey," Pita told him. "Honey from the wild bee tree, remember?" Slowly Paco nodded. "I think I remember. A little," he said.

Mama went on talking. "These cakes are called *tortillitas de regale.* They are an old, old kind of sweet cake. My grandmother taught me to make them a long time ago. Today we had everything we needed once we got the honey and the piñons and the Trader found the bottle of orange water in his pack."

Mama took the tin that was filled with sweet cakes from the fireplace coals. Quickly she emptied it on the bench where she was working. "Your Tía Pita," laughingly she said to Paco, "took my table for her *Niño* shrine, but a bench is just as good if it's covered with a clean flour sack." Mama laughed again. She was very happy. The Posada would be a good fiesta. "Here, Paco, have a *tortillita de regale.* You know why we call them by this name? It is because they are little gift tortillas eaten for pleasure. Good, no?"

"Good!" Paco answered and reached for a handful.

There was a knock at the door. Justin and José had come to help build the Christmas *luminarios.* Paco had never made them before. So now the three boys went outdoors to build them. The boys brought a sackful of small pine sticks, heavy with resin. With these, they built knee-high towers of four sticks laid in a square and other fours added to them. They built the stick towers along both sides of the pathway from the portal to the gate. Tonight, before the Holy Family and the pilgrims came, Paco would light each one. The glowing *luminarios* would light the way of welcome to the door of his home.

Soon the Maestro came with the shouting younger children of his morning school. They had brought sackfuls of pine needles with them. All morning they had gone up and down the snowy mountain-side whacking branches from the pine trees and stripping them of their needles. Now they shoveled all the snow from the pathway. Then they spread the path with the spicy

139

smelling needles. This would make the green way, the way of welcome for Mary and Joseph to walk upon.

The winter sun had set and the evening wind moaned in the canyons. The snowy world seemed bathed in blue light. The air turned blue and cold, the freezing blue of winter, the freezing cold of winter.

The school children went home. They ploughed through the snow-filled streets to eat their suppers, to get on their Sunday clothes and to come back with their parents for La Posada.

Justin and José went into the lean-to with Paco, to help him feed the burro and to feed and milk the cow. Pita could have all of the milk that was milked tonight. Carmen would not need her share, and the Padre had said that now his cat was gone, his liking for milk also had gone.

Finally Justin and José went home. Paco put the wild dog's supper outside his bedroom door and went into the house.

A line of black-shawled women passed him, walking slowly across the yard and through the gate. Abuela and Carmen were with them.

Pita called the Trader and Paco to a supper of blue corn tortillas and thick, sweet, cinnamon-flavored chocolate. As he ate, Paco looked around at the pretty room decorated with branches and sprays of mountain greens. The shrine of the *Santo Niño* was in the shad-

140

ows. Even the bright fire in the fireplace did not light it, but he could see dimly the outline of the *Santo Niño*.

"That's the *Santo Niño* from the church," he said. "Who brought it? When did it come?"

"The ladies of the Society of Mary. They always bring the *Santo Niño* to the house of La Posada every year. They passed you as you came in," Pita answered.

"Aren't there candles for His place?" Paco asked. "It is so dark. No one can see the Holy Child."

Pita told him, "There are candles. Mary and Joseph will light them when the time is right. This is the way of La Posada."

"I have seen many Posadas," the Trader said, "in many villages here and in Mexico. They are the same except in small ways. In small ways they differ a little. In some places the Christ Child waits in the church for His mother's coming."

Pita was surprised. "Here the ladies bring Him to the chosen house. Mary takes Him back to the church when she goes to the midnight Mass."

"Listen," Paco whispered. Softly, far away they could hear the people singing. Then he shouted, "They are coming. They are coming."

"Not yet." Pita smiled at him. "They must stop at eight houses along the way. Eight houses keep their doors shut tight before they come to this house. We

141

have time before they get here to put on our Sunday clothes. Set fire to the *luminarios,* Paco, so that they will light the way."

Paco went outside to light the Christmas fires. He looked at the wild dog's supper dish. The food had been eaten, but the wild dog was nowhere near. Then Paco went to his room to put on the suit Tomás had bought him to wear at Pita's wedding.

When he came back into the kitchen the Trader was there, shining clean and wearing a new woven poncho. "Found it in my packsack," the Trader said proudly. Paco grinned. That packsack seemed to be a treasure sack.

Pita came into the room. She was wearing her wedding dress and earrings from her wedding chest. She had been beautiful on her wedding day. She was beautiful every day, but tonight she was more than beautiful. Paco's breath caught. "Oh, if Tío Tomás would come so he could see you," he cried. Instantly he was sorry he had said it for he saw tears in the beautiful Tía Pita's eyes.

The singing was plainer now. Joseph sang:

> There is no room at the inn.
> Open your house door, I pray you,
> To give Mary shelter.

143

Inside the house the people sang:

> There is no room here.
> This door is closed
> to you, a stranger.

The pilgrims sang:

> Give shelter.
> We pray you
> Give shelter to the Mother
> And the Holy Infant.

The people sang:

> We know you not.
> You may be thieves and robbers.
> Be on your way.
> This door is closed.

Paco could hear the prayers that they chanted as Mary and Joseph and the Pilgrims moved onward.

At last they stopped at the eighth house. The songs were sung. The door remained closed. The procession moved on.

Soon there was movement in the yard of the house of Tío Tomás. There was a knock at the door. Joseph's voice rang out into the stillness of the night:

> There is no room at the inn.
> Open the house door, I pray you
> To give Mary shelter.

Inside the house, Pita's soft voice rang clear and true. The Trader's voice rang clear and strong. Paco's voice was but a whisper, but he sang with them.

> The door stands open
> For Mary
> And for the Christ Child
> Who is to be born.
> The door stands open.
> Enter.

Mary came in, and Joseph was with her, and the Pilgrims were there. In back of them came the people of Santa María-of-the-Gardens.

The Padre opened his book and from it he read the holy words:

> And lo the angels of the Lord came upon them and the glory of the Lord shone round about them. . . . And the Angels said unto them, Fear not, for behold I bring you good tidings of great joy . . . for in the town of David is born this day a Saviour which is Christ the Lord. . . .

Pita came across the room with two candles which she handed to Mary and Joseph. Taking them, they went to the place where the image of the *Santo Niño* waited for them. They went to light the candles at His shrine.

145

But they stopped. There was shouting in the yard. There was a knock at the door. Silently, quickly Pita ran to the door with Carmen beside her. They ran to the door and opened it. Tomás and Carlos came into the room.

FOR a small second the candles were forgotten while Pita and Tomás and Paco and Carmen and Carlos looked at one another with hearts full of gladness, but without words.

Then the candles were lighted. The holy part of La Posada was over.

Mama and her younger daughters, the wife of the Postmaster and the wife of the Storekeeper passed plates of *tortillitas de regale* and cups of thick sweet chocolate to Mary and Joseph and the Pilgrims and to all the people of Santa María-of-the-Gardens. Paco gave chocolate and sweet tortillas to the Padre, to the father of Tomás and to the father of Pita. He would have liked to listen to what Tomás was telling Pita, but he had a duty to perform. He had a responsibility to fulfill. This was his house and these were his honored guests.

Pita and Carmen, Tomás and Carlos were talking quietly. But they were not talking of the month of separation. They were not talking of the dangers on the homeward trip. They were talking of La Posada. They were talking of this night when the *Santo Niño* had been welcomed.

Tomás said sadly, "We came with empty hands, my Pita. We could not get our bundles through the snow in the Pass."

"But look," Carlos said excitedly, "they did not need paper for the paper flowers. Look around you. Is this not beautiful what they brought from the mountain? They did not need cookies that are bought in packages nor sweet water that comes in bottles. Have you not tasted, Tomás, the *tortillitas* and the chocolate?"

"Carlos is right, María Pita. Everything is so beautiful and so good. How did you manage it?"

Pita smiled at Tomás. "It was Paco's dream," she said.

"Paco's dream?" Tomás did not understand. He called to Paco. "What is this about your dream, young Paco? Come tell us. Come tell us about this dream."

But Paco could not tell him. "I think it was a dream," he said, "or partly so. I can't remember, Tío Tomás." Paco was embarrassed. It bothered him that he could not answer what Tío Tomás asked of him.

Tomás did not want to embarrass the boy or to tease him. He said to Pita, "Come, María Pita. I have not even a gift for the Christ Child, but we will kneel and offer our happiness for His Christmas gift."

151

Together they walked across the room—the proud, tall Tomás and the beautiful Pita. They knelt before the shrine. Pita bowed her head. Tomás, being taller, saw something move at the feet of the *Santo Niño*. He leaned forward for a closer look. He reached forward to poke a gentle finger at something there.

Purring loudly, the Padre's cat jumped down. Behind her at the feet of the Christ Child she left her Christmas gift, her newborn kitten.

Paco saw it. He exclaimed in surprise. "Ah, Tío Tomás, Tía Pita. I remember my dream."

Everyone pressed forward to see the kitten and to hear the story of the dream. The Padre picked up his cat from the floor and held her in his arms. He had thought she was lost. He had thought something had happened to her. The cat purred loudly.

Paco was talking. It was hard to talk with all the people looking at him, listening to what he said. It was hard to remember backward and yet, now, the dream was very clear.

"And so after a while I went to sleep." He looked at Pita. Not for worlds would he tell anyone that she had cried. "And then . . . this part is the dream, I think. The animals came around me. They made a circle around me. They spoke. I think they spoke. There was the bear and the deer. There was the pack rat and the

153

jack rabbit. There were other animals, too, the wild dog, the Padre's cat, Tía Carmen's cow and the Trader's burro."

Paco stopped. Everyone listened. No one laughed. The boy began to talk again. "There they were, my friends, all the animals. They talked to me. The deer said, 'You have no paper for paper flowers? How foolish! I will give you something more beautiful than paper flowers.' The bear said, 'You have no sugar for sweet cakes? How foolish! I will give you something far sweeter.' The pack rat said, 'You know what I have. Take it. It is yours.' The jack rabbit told me, 'Follow my tracks in the snow. I will lead where you should go.'"

Paco stopped again. He was not used to so much talking. Pita smiled at him. She gave him strength and courage. "So I left my bed. I took my blanket and I followed the jack rabbit's tracks." He stopped again. He laughed. He said, "Now I think the dream stops here and the true things happened. It was very cold, but I did not seem to mind the cold. I followed the jack rabbit's tracks. I followed them up the mountain. When I came to the deer's retreat, my friend the deer was there. He gave me the blue spruce and the cedar berries, the mistletoe and the kinni-kinnick. Then I followed the jack rabbit to the wild bee tree. My

friend, the bear, was there. He gave me honey. The pack rat emptied his nest of piñon nuts. He said they were all for me."

The boy looked at Pita. He was silent for a long time. He said, "Tía Pita, help me, will you? I think that here the dream began again. I was very tired. I was very cold. I rested a while and the cow down in the valley called up to me. She called, 'Come home, Paco. You have my milk for the Posada guests.' The burro called up to me, 'Come home, Paco. The things in my pack saddle are for you. Come home or I will come and get you.' The Padre's cat called up to me, 'I have a gift for the Christ Child, Paco. Come home. Come home.'"

Pita sobbed. Tomás touched her hand. She said softly, "Let me finish, Paco. The dream ends here again and true things happened. The wild dog, your dog, came to my door for me and the Trader's burro. The three of us—your dog, the burrito and I—brought you home with the gifts you had for the *Santo Niño* and for me."

There was silence. The fire in the fireplace crackled. The cat in the Padre's arms purred. Then all the people spoke. They spoke with one voice. It rang loudly in the quiet room. "Miracle. Paco's miracle."

The Padre spoke. "Paco's miracle," he said. "Yes. A miracle has taken place. A miracle of understanding.

Paco, here, now knows that kindness and gentleness is the language of the heart that can be understood by all God's creatures. It does not need to be expressed with words. And you, my children, have learned to value the gentle way of living. You have seen that happiness is to be found here on your own mountain and in your own valley."

The priest put his hand on Paco's shoulder, but he spoke to his people. "A miracle, yes, but one that has been happening every day. It has been happening before your eyes, but you could not see it."

Then, stooping to tilt Paco's face upward so that he could look into the young boy's eyes, he said, "Has no one ever told you that Paco is not a name? It is a nickname. It is the small name for Francisco. Your real name is Francisco."

"San Francisco," Pita murmured.

"Saint Francis," the Maestro said. "Saint Francis of Assisi."

But above all the voices, Paco heard the Old One talking. He heard the words Pierre had told him over and over and over. "This is your heritage. Be true to your name."

At last it had happened. The sign he had longed for had been given to him. The animals loved him. They understood him—perhaps not his words, but his heart.

157

Now he knew he could fulfill the Old One's dream.

The Padre spoke, "It is time for the midnight Mass of Christmas. Let the procession be started."

The people formed in line. The Trader brought his burro from the lean-to. He spoke to Mary and to the image she carried. "To honor us," he said. Mary nodded. "To honor you," she answered.

Joseph helped her up upon the burro's back. He gave the lead rope to Paco. Paco looked at the Trader. The Trader nodded. "You lead them, Paco," he said. "I will stay at home to guard the hearth fire."

Paco looked into the shadows. He saw the wild dog lying by his bedroom door. It would guard the hearth fire. "My dog will guard the house," he said to the Trader.

The people began singing the song of Christmas. Slowly the procession went down the snow-filled street, across the plaza to the Church of Santa María and to Christmas Mass.